D1509811

KGEBETLI MOELE

# The Book of the Dead

Kwela Books

To Tonono and Mothlatlego
Thanks for playing the role

Kwela Books,
an imprint of NB Publishers,
40 Heerengracht, Cape Town, South Africa
PO Box 6525, Roggebaai, 8012, South Africa
www.kwela.com

Cover image by Pieter Hugo
(courtesy of the artist and Michael Stevenson/Cape Town)
Cover design by Michiel Botha
Author photograph by Lisa Skinner
Typography by Nazli Jacobs
Set in Stone Serif
Printed and bound by Paarl Print,
Oosterland Street, Paarl, South Africa

First edition, first impression 2009

ISBN: 978-0-7957-0288-4

"Don't inject me with that venom."

Thabo "Nyakza" Matsane

# Book of the Living

# 1

He, Khutso, had been many things in his life. He had been a child, a teenager, a young man, a husband and a father. But the one thing he had never been was happy; he had never enjoyed his life. He knew the odds and he fought them. He had his dreams and he chased them. He had his goals and he worked hard to achieve them. But Khutso had never enjoyed his life; he had only ever endured the struggle that his life had been. There had never been a moment in his life that he felt fulfilled, that he felt true happiness, that he felt joy. There were always things in the way. Things to live up to: wants, needs, wishes.

# 2

Masakeng – the place where Khutso grew up – was a village where only one house had electricity and a borehole. Most of the community relied on water from the springs that they shared with their animals, unless they had five cents to buy a twenty-five-litre bottle of water from the local businessman – who owned the house with the borehole – or if they had the energy to walk more than ten kilometres to a government-supplied tap.

The home of the businessman was the centre of the community. Next door to the house was his shop/café and hardware store, which also acted as a post office – though letters could only be picked up there, not posted. Inside was the only television in the village, and every Saturday it was the hottest spot in the community, especially if there was a game between Chiefs and Pirates.

To any outsider this was a boring place, a place caught in time, but to the natives who had left for the big cities it was even worse – and when they came back they no doubt justified their visit by telling themselves that they were home to visit their ancestors; to give thanks, to ask for a better tomorrow. But for their families, those who had been left behind, their return was a chance to display their relatives' achievements for all to see. And so it was that every year end, when people came back home for the Christmas holidays, the well-to-do families in the village had endless parties.

Khutso used to enjoy the parties immensely as a child. With his friends Ngwan'Zo and Maoto he would enjoy the good food – the bucket of home-made juice and cookies that melted away in one's mouth – and the occasional beer that they would steal or an irresponsible adult would give them. And it was at one of these parties, after listening to the old people reminiscing about all that had happened when they were still young, that the gramophone had begun to sing and they had started to dance.

Khutso always loved dancing because even at that young age he had the ability to impress everyone – even the women would stop what they were doing to watch Khutso dance. In fact, people loved his dancing so much that he would instantly become a member of that family.

However, as Khutso grew up he began to notice that in some homes, including his own, nobody came back for the holidays – his sisters never came home with their husbands and his brothers didn't come home with their wives. For Khutso, Christmas was something that took place in other households.

The following Christmas Khutso was sad and angry. He was supposed to attend a party at the house of one of the well-off families, and his mother wanted him to wash first, but because there were no new clothes or new shoes to wear that Christmas he saw no reason to do what she told him.

Later, at the party, a man looked at him strangely. Khutso awoke memories of himself at that age – he remembered wearing a pair of over-sized khaki shorts that his mother had retailored a dozen times (shorts his elder brothers had probably worn before he was even born). "There are crocodiles in the water," the man said. "I know."

"Crocodiles?" Khutso responded, missing his point.

"I used to be just as you are, and I believe that you are going to grow up to be as I am," the man said, remembering that he only started washing when he got to the city of gold. Then he smiled and gave Khutso five cents because he had run out of words.

That morning Khutso felt sad that he didn't have new clothes, but as the day progressed his sadness slowly ebbed away – after all, he thought, his friends were in the same predicament.

They ate and had a little to drink and then they were asked to dance. They danced, thrilling everyone, and some of the guests showed their appreciation by giving Khutso money, patting him on the shoulder as they did so. Overflowing with confidence, Khutso took advantage of the fact that a grandchild of the host family had been impressed by his moves. Oblivious to the fact that she was an urban girl – born and bred – he asked her if they could walk to the gate together. The girl saw no problem, and although he did not know what he was going to say to her, the fact that she had agreed to go to the gate with him made Khutso think that she was his.

"I love you," he told her as they walked past the cars, heading towards the gate.

She smiled and laughed, a little surprised by the sudden words.

"I love you," Khutso continued. "Can I kiss you?"

He kissed her without waiting for a response.

"Hoo!" she exhaled, pushing him back. "Are you sick? Take a good look at yourself."

Suddenly she was shouting, and pretty soon she had almost everyone's attention.

"Look at me and then look at yourself . . . Who do you think you are?" she asked, looking him in the eye. "I asked you a question. Who do you think you are?" Then she slapped him so hard that he fell on the ground.

It didn't help matters that he had summoned his friends Ngwan'Zo and Maoto, telling them that he was going to teach them how to handle girls. They saw him fall and laughed hard, clapping their hands.

After that Khutso went out of his way to avoid celebrations of any kind and he never wanted to dance – his ego had been bruised irreparably.

* * *

In the days that followed his humiliation at the party, Khutso tried to understand why it was that certain families always celebrated Christmas and certain families did not. After much contemplation, he finally put it to his mother, hoping that she would give him the answer.

"These people have parties and cars because they can afford them," Khutso's mother told him. "And they can afford them because they are educated." She stopped what she was doing and looked into the distance because she could not bear to look at the pain on her child's face. "Your father was not educated," she finally revealed. "And your mother did not get herself educated either. There were other things that interested her more."

What she didn't say was that she had been a promising pupil at school, she had never failed even a test, but school hadn't held her attention. She had been more interested in boys and the futile game of life – she thought that life was like a game, where you run around trying to win it – and because of that she didn't even have Standard One.

Her husband too had been respected by his schoolteachers because of his mathematical abilities, but he was also revered by his fellow pupils for his skill with the soccer ball. He was a phenomenon, as soccer players are rarely good mathematicians, but his hope was to be a professional soccer player and after primary school he gave schoolbooks no second thought. She remembered his words while he was still alive:

"Education is for foolish people, you teach them and examine them on what you have taught them, and then, when they pass the exam, they feel that opportunities will come their way, respect and all . . ."

He made opportunities come his way in another way – he became a striker for Pirates, a career that lasted nearly three seasons – and everything was milk and honey until his name was called. His family's hopes had died with him. Khutso had arrived two months after he was buried, and his mother had named him Khutso because that was what he brought to her: peace. She was left all alone to scrabble together a life for her big family – she had given birth to seven healthy children before the age of twenty-five – so she took her family from Soweto and came back to Masakeng, where her husband had been building them a house. There they lived in it as it stood – unfinished.

* * *

After what his mother had told him, Khutso began the next school year filled with determination fuelled by anger – he wanted to be educated so that he could have new clothes at Christmas and parties at his house. "My son," his mother told him on the first day of the new term, "I, your mother, want you to be educated because: One, your mother didn't go past Standard One. And, two, because I want you to be a man within this community. I want you to be a man within this nation. Then you can have your own cars, and throw your own parties, and have a wardrobe so big that you don't have to wash your clothes for a whole year. Khutso, promise me that you will go to school."

"I promise."

"I want you to become an educated man," she said. "Promise that you will become a doctor."

"I promise."

14

Khutso's mother didn't have money for many things, but from that day on, because of his promise, she always paid his school fees on time, and she made sure that he had school shoes and a uniform, that he washed every night before sleeping and that in the morning he had soft porridge or yesterday's leftovers before he went to class.

# 3

In primary school Khutso never bunked once, even though Thaba-kgolo Primary School was a nine kilometres' walk from his home, but after a couple of years at Lehlasedi High School his sporadic attendance began to worry his teachers. He always started the new school year in the same way – with a deep desire to go to school – but by the time the first school holidays came around, being at school had drained his energy. School is boring, he would think to himself. But in Standard Eight Khutso and his friends started smoking dagga, and after the first holidays – when his willpower was at its weakest – he began bunking school.

It started with him failing to submit his homework. After that he didn't attend the subjects in which he still had to complete his work. Then he began to bunk school every Friday, telling himself that he would make up the lost days later in the term. But he never did and so he was behind in all his subjects. His teachers, who really believed in him, tried to understand what was wrong, but Khutso would just promise to attend class and they quickly came to learn that he never kept his promises.

Khutso bunked the whole of the second and third school terms that year and only came back to school a month into the final term. Unsurprisingly, to the disappointment of his mother, he failed Standard Eight.

\* \* \*

The greatest influence and inspiration in the community was Leruo, the son of the local businessman. They said that his father had had no formal schooling and that he had taught himself to read and write. Whatever the truth, everyone knew that Leruo's father had worked in the city of gold for a long time before coming back home to the village to open the café and hardware store.

Leruo, like all his siblings, had been to the most exclusive schools. And just like his brothers and sisters he had dropped out of university, but his father hadn't minded at all. "Education can do nothing for you, which is why I left school. In this life you don't need education to live, you only need brains," he'd said to his son.

Leruo's father had worked hard and made enough money to build the only double-storey house in the dusty community, the only house with a borehole, and although all his children had dropped out of university, he was sure that they would live far better lives than he and his father had lived.

"Look at the people teaching you . . ." he'd said to his son. "If education improves people's lives, then why aren't their lives improved in any way? They are slaves to the government. And look at those who have retired, people who have educated others for years and years, they are still poor."

Leruo continued from where his old man had hung up. He had a fleet of taxis and a brick-manufacturing company, had more than thirty people working for him, but despite his wealth he was still a man of the people.

Usually, when the well-educated came back from university they behaved like strangers in the community. They thought of themselves as better than everyone else, and would quickly start to complain about how boring the place was. It was obvious to everyone that they were only home to show people how successful they had become. But Leruo was different. He talked to people in the community, and would always help if his hand was wanted.

However, Leruo was also part of Khutso's problem. He loved temporary labour and paid cash at the end of the working day. By bunking school and working for Leruo, Khutso could feed his new-found hobbies – smoking and drinking. His money was the main reason that Khutso began bunking school.

* * *

Khutso thought he knew everything, thought that he had everything under control, that with his friends, Ngwan'Zo and Maoto, he was invincible. To him it was as if they were one. These were the boys that he had learned everything with: They were the boys that he had played with since he had started to walk. They had started at primary school and continued high school together. They had gone to komeng together and had come out of komeng – as men – together. They had shared their first bottle of alcohol together. They had learned to smoke together. But in their third year at high school things changed. In the first quarter of the new school year, Ngwan'Zo quit school after beating up his class teacher. The teacher had slapped him in the face and he had retaliated, then the cops were called and even though the governors of the school tried to intervene, they couldn't stop Ngwan'Zo quitting school.

Maoto followed in his footsteps two months later. He got into a fight with the same teacher his friend had fought with, and as it was with his friend so it was with him. People in the know believed that Khutso would end up fighting the teacher as well, and also quit school, but Khutso respected all his teachers and they never failed to try to lead him in the right direction. In fact, Khutso even tried to convince his friends that they should come back to school. "You should apologise," he told them. "Then we could go through high school together. It's boring without you." But they never listened to him.

*  *  *

When they were high, Khutso and his friends used to tell each other that they were going to have the greatest law firm in the world. They told each other that their law firm's headquarters would be in their own village; that they would pack the village's poverty into a container and export it to foreign lands. Then they would pave every road and every footpath. "Not construct new footpaths," Ngwan'Zo said, exhaling smoke and looking at it as it disappeared into the air, "but pave the existing footpaths, keeping them the way our life here has engineered them."

"And we won't name the streets," Khutso added. "They should remain as nameless as they are."

Maoto laughed in a muted way. "We will also build our own school," he said, smiling at the thought.

"Schools," Ngwan'Zo corrected him. "Primary school, high school and a University of Masakeng."

If they were not building magnificent castles in the air, Khutso would skip school and together the three of them would load one of Leruo's six-cubic-metre tipper trucks for fifteen cents per load. While they worked they would sing songs composed on demand, songs whose beats were derived from the rhythm of their shovels as they were shoved into the river sand. It always made the work easier.

These songs always carried strong messages, but somehow they never listened to the messages, or maybe they just chose not to.

| QUESTION: | *Heh! Ngwan'Zo, what is your problem? Why aren't you going to school?* |
|---|---|
| CHORUS: | *Because I beat my very own teacher.* |
| | *I beat him up, I beat him up.* |
| QUESTION: | *Why did you beat him up? Do you know what you did to your future?* |
| RESPONSE: | *No. I can't tell you until the case has been resolved in the High Court.* |
| CHORUS: | *Because I beat my very own teacher.* |
| | *I beat him up, I beat him up.* |
| RESPONSE: | *My future is as good as what I do in a pit toilet: fucked-up shit.* |
| CHORUS: | *Because I beat my very own teacher.* |
| | *I beat him up, I beat him up.* |

Ngwan'Zo had composed the song himself and he liked it more than any other, and, in fact, it became so popular that when the initiates were coming out of komeng that year it was the song they sang.

\* \* \*

Leruo was a source of hope to Khutso and his friends because he always made them believe that they could be whatever they wanted to be in life, even though, like a responsible adult, he tried to show them the light. "So your time to bunk school has come," he said to Khutso when it became clear that he had given up on education. "But something beats me about you, you always went to school like a model pupil, then you just sort of lost interest. Why?"

"There is no money at school," Khutso said, uninterestedly.

Leruo looked at him with a strange smile, then he looked into the distance.

"Tell him," Ngwan'Zo said. "Tell him that whoever needs money has to work hard for it."

"I need people to work for me," Leruo finally replied, "but I am still going to tell you to go to school. We are not all cut out to be rich people, but education will make you a better human being. And you will be thankful that you got an education when you had the time to."

"Leruo, everybody is always preaching that we should go to school," Ngwan'Zo said, "but most of them didn't go to school themselves."

"Do you want to know why?" Leruo asked him.

"Why?"

"It's because they had the chance to go to school, and like you they didn't take the opportunity. Now they are feeling the disadvantages of not having an education."

"Why do you think they didn't take the opportunity?"

"Because they thought that they knew better, just like you."

"That's a lie," Ngwan'Zo said. "If that were true they would go to adult education classes and get educated."

"Well, I am always thinking that I should go back to university," Leruo said, "but I can't afford to leave my businesses and go and study again. That part of my life is over."

Khutso forgot about the conversation until one night when his mother cornered him.

"Khutso," she said, looking at her last-born son, "I have always wanted you to go to university and be a doctor, and I have worked hard so that you can go to school, so I am going to give you another chance, the same as I gave all your brothers and sisters."

His mother had never been able to give her children the opportunities that Leruo's father had given his sons and daughters, but she had always made sure that whatever else had happened they had always gone to school.

"Don't you think that your brothers and sisters are crying when they think how much of my energy they have wasted, how much of my hard-earned money they have thrown away?" his mother asked Khutso. "They know that I am poor. They know I wanted better things for them. They know, and yet still your sisters keep dumping their children on me, still your brothers keep asking me for money." Tears filled the old woman's eyes as she looked at Khutso. "They say that you can take a horse to the water but you can't make it drink," she went on, wiping away her tears. "But I am telling you, Khutso, to use this chance. Don't throw it away like your brothers and sisters did before you."

Khutso's mother could not bring herself to disown her own children; she had always given them one more chance, and they had always disappointed her. Khutso's eldest brother had just quit school one day, deciding that he wanted to become a taxi driver. But after his mother had sacrificed to get him a driver's licence and saved enough for a deposit on a taxi, he had disappointed her – he never brought anything home. Three years later he had run the taxi into the ground, so he sold it and arrived home after a few months with nothing at all. "This is your home, you are welcome to stay," Khutso's mother had told him, "but please don't ever ask for anything again."

A few months later he got a job as a taxi driver in the big city and moved out. They hadn't seen him again, but sometimes he would send a letter asking for money.

Khutso's four sisters kept bringing home fatherless children. His mother tried again and again to put them back in school, but it was never long before they arrived home with yet another baby. And to top it all they never got married; they just moved in with their boyfriends.

This was a source of great pain to Khutso's mother, because she couldn't visit them or recognise her extended families as they had never been introduced in the traditional way.

* * *

That night Khutso lay in his bed thinking of all the things that his mother had done for his brothers and sisters, for his sisters' children and for him. He thought about what Leruo had said to Ngwan'Zo, and then he thought about all the things that his teachers had said to him. Finally, he thought about all the money that he and his friends had made shifting sand. The most they had ever moved in a day was eight loads, and although it was good money – that day they had celebrated by buying sardines, baked beans, spaghetti, atchar and a litre of soft drink – they had always smoked and drunk the rest of whatever they had earned over the following weekend. The money that Leruo paid them was always spent in the shebeen. He had never done anything good with it.

Khutso thought about the people in the community that he considered happy, and concluded that they were happy because they had money. He saw that money could buy you everything in this world – respect, love and happiness. I have to make money, he told himself. If I want to have friends, have the freshest-looking face, and be respected left, right and centre, I have to make money. And Khutso wanted to be respected and adored. He dreamed of it. And he wanted to have friends. That's all he ever wanted.

Then Khutso looked at the options that he had, and after pondering them all he came up with a way out: school. It was the only solution he was sure about. He had never really been the brightest, but with some hard work he was sure he could succeed. School is like a railway line,

23

he thought to himself. The train that runs on the rails has but one destination, and if it runs smoothly, sure enough it will reach its destination at the expected time. He knew he could work hard – he'd worked hard for Leruo, shovelling sand – but he also knew that people who work hard are the worst paid of all and that to get paid very well one has to have a degree.

# 4

There were many steps that Khutso took to try and get away from Ngwan'Zo and Maoto, but whenever he tried to shave them off he found himself remembering how free and happy he felt when he was with them. Without them he felt like something nocturnal caught in daylight.

In class, Khutso would long to be with his friends. The biology teacher would be delivering his lesson, but Khutso would be filled with the feeling that he was missing out on something important. He had no doubt that Ngwan'Zo and Maoto were up to something magical and magnificent while he was stuck in the classroom. It was then that he would sneak out of school and try to find them.

Khutso tried and failed to get away from his friends until the Saturday that Mashego's last-born son was initiated.

Mashego, not wanting to be outdone by the wealthy families in the community, celebrated his son's introduction to manhood by slaughtering a bull. In addition, there was a never-ending supply of alcohol. The guests started with traditional beer and moved on to all sorts of modern liquor, and late at night there was even brandy.

It was after the brandy that Ngwan'Zo managed to drag a drunken girl, who was five times over her limit, out of the party. Together, they herded her into a deserted house. There Maoto took his turn with her, then Ngwan'Zo, and afterwards, as she was lying on the floor, passed out, Khutso was unwillingly forced on top of her to take a turn.

Later, shame came over Khutso – shame that he had taken part in the act and enjoyed it. He wanted to go to the girl and apologise, but the shame choked him. He knew he wouldn't even be able to look at her.

But, unlike Khutso, Maoto and Ngwan'Zo revelled in what they had done – talking about it triumphantly and laughing victoriously. They mocked Khutso about the act and in the end it was this that guaranteed the end of their friendship. One day Khutso just stopped hanging around with them, and this time he didn't miss them.

*   *   *

Khutso had always thought of himself as the friendliest of people, but without Maoto and Ngwan'Zo he soon discovered that he was just not a sociable person. He found it hard to make new friends, and in the end he became friends with the classroom and its work. It was then that he discovered that books were much friendlier than people.

That year Khutso passed Standard Eight, which he was doing for the second time, relatively easily, and his mother wondered at the change in him, because he would spend weekend after weekend at home without once going out of the gate.

The following year he went on to pass Standard Nine at his first attempt, and in his Standard Ten year his mother prayed every night as Khutso sat at the kitchen table consuming book after book.

*   *   *

Khutso could not wait to write his final examinations – he was confident – but afterwards, although he knew that he had done very well, his anxiety reached a new level as he waited for the schools to reopen in the new year so that he could get his results. And, yes, he had done very well. He had the best results in the school. In fact, he had topped the whole circuit, and his teachers wanted him to go to a training college, because with a B in mathematics in the higher grade he could teach the subject in any school – even his own mathematics teacher only had a D in the higher grade.

Khutso's anxiety turned into fear, his thought processes overheating. He wasn't sure of anything. He wasn't sure what he wanted to do with his future. His teachers were only talking. There was nothing concrete in what they were saying, and Khutso knew that passing matric so well was the equivalent of exposing one's family as poor – he knew that his mother would never be able to pay for him to attend college. So, with that thought in his head, he slowly dragged his feet home.

At home, his mother was so excited that she couldn't contain herself. She hugged and kissed him like she used to when he was still a toddler, long ago. She kissed him till it became an embarrassment to him. "I never had one of these," she said, holding up his statement of results. "Your father never had one either, and your brothers and sisters . . . none of them ever had a matric certificate."

Then his mother danced a ritual dance, thanking all of her ancestors because she had never believed that she would ever hold a matric certificate in her hands.

* * *

Late that night, after the celebrations had died down and all her grandchildren were sleeping, his mother called Khutso to the kitchen table. He had been rolling about in his bed, fighting hard not to cry, his thoughts running into cul-de-sac after cul-de-sac, but when he got to the table his thoughts froze. There was money on it. More money than he ever thought his mother could save.

His mother looked at him, wiping away happy tears. "I am crying," she said, trying to compose herself. "I am crying because I am happy. I

27

never thought we would see this day. I thought that you were going to turn out just like your brothers. I am very happy today that you have passed your Standard Ten so well. I am so happy that I am crying."

She took her time composing herself and her thoughts. "Here is all the money that I was saving for you," she finally said. "What are you going to do with it?"

"They say that I should go to teacher-training college."

"What are you saying?"

"I want to go to college."

"Do they produce doctors at college?"

"No, they only produce teachers."

"And where do they produce doctors?"

"University."

She paused and looked at him. "Khutso, I want you to be a doctor,' she said. "Go to the University of the North and come back a doctor, my child. Forget about being a teacher. You have finished with school. Go to the university. I am asking you to go to university and be a doctor."

# 5

Khutso was admitted to the University of the North, but the university didn't produce medical doctors, so Khutso enrolled to study law. His mother didn't mind, he was a student at the University of the North and that was all that mattered to her.

The library was the first thing that he wanted to see when he arrived at the university. He had read about libraries – places full of books – and they fascinated him because he had never been inside one. Back at home, before his journey, he had decided that he would read each and every book in the university library.

Following the directions to the library, he soon found himself outside it. He stopped, his excitement growing as he looked at it, wondering how many books – books that he was going to read – were inside.

Inside the library he wanted to scream – his mouth wide open – totally amazed by even the few books that he could see. He covered his mouth with his hand. This wasn't what he had thought the library would be. He had thought that he would read all the books in the shortest time . . . He had thought that it would be the size of a classroom.

Still smiling, Khutso sank down onto the floor, shaking his head, defeated by his thoughts. "I am in a library," he said quietly to himself, his eyes filling with tears.

* * *

Later that afternoon Khutso found himself sitting with his roommate, Tshepo, in front of their residential block, carefully observing the student life that they had just joined. There were many beautiful young women at the university, and Khutso looked at them, knowing that Tshepo was doing the same.

"I never had a girlfriend in high school," Tshepo said, revealing something from his past.

But Khutso didn't answer him, and so they just sat there, looking at the student life that was passing them by on their first Friday as students of the University of the North.

"I think I should not have a girlfriend here as well," Tshepo added after some time, but still Khutso did not say anything.

"I think I will just try to be a student one hundred per cent, just like I was a pupil one hundred per cent. I always wanted a girlfriend. I thought about it constantly. But, truthfully, having a girlfriend would mess up my work. She would be a hindrance to my academic advancement."

"Women, my dear roommate," Khutso said cryptically.

"Did you have girlfriends in high school?" Tshepo asked.

"I had my fair share," Khutso lied. "They are nothing, dear roommate, but I see what you're saying. They can be a problem, and I think I will also take an academic break from the game of breaking hearts, because my dreams are on the line here."

But before the end of their second week at university Khutso had seen a young woman who stirred something deep inside him. When he looked at her, his heartbeat changed, and the very fact that she made his heart beat faster scared him, which in turn made his heart beat even faster.

The first time he had seen her had been in the lecture hall.

"Sorry, I am late," she had said, closing the door quietly behind her.

Immediately, the packed hall had gone dead quiet. "What's your name, young lady?" the lecturer, who had been struggling to gain control of the students, had asked her.

"Pretty," she replied.

# 6

Pretty, as the name suggests, was pretty. Girls like her were not for marriage but for show, so people believed. They believed that her kind were made for sharing amongst men, as no one man could ever handle such beauty alone without jealousy rendering him insane.

Pretty had her first boyfriend in Standard One. Every morning a man came to deliver his boss's children to school and there they would find her at the gate. One morning, the man asked her to choose between his boss's three sons. She chose Lehlogonolo, the eldest son, as they were in the same class, and with that she guaranteed herself half of Lehlogonolo's lunchbox, which for a poor girl was luxury. Though she shared his lunchbox every day, she only kissed Lehlogonolo once – and that was in the presence of the driver, who had coached him – but this became the foundation of what she knew her beauty could do for her.

As she grew older Pretty learned quickly that her beauty scared men out of their minds, but she also learned that men don't deserve to be trusted.

Only once had she trusted a man. Her Standard Four class teacher was someone she could talk to. She thought of him as a second father, as he appeared to be the only person in her world who was concerned about her.

She trusted him until one Friday afternoon when she found her back flat on his bed, her legs spread, her body racked with excruciating pain.

"Please don't tell anybody," he said afterwards as he put money in her hand.

And she didn't tell anybody. Not because she didn't want to tell her story, but because she never knew how to start telling or to whom she would tell it.

Monday came and some more currency was paid. She did not know what to say. Then Friday came around again and another appointment was made. Her legs took her to his quarters on Saturday, and there were new shoes and a beautiful miniskirt that she had to wear there and then. Dressed in the new clothes, she looked at herself in the mirror and for the first time in her life she saw herself as if she were looking through someone else's eyes and was overwhelmed by her own beauty.

Then people started talking about her. She was a poor girl wearing expensive clothes, and it wasn't long before the truth was exposed. Then the teacher tried to distance himself from her, but he couldn't keep away. He tried to be discreet, but there were eyes that saw and tongues that wagged and waggled until the authorities could no longer continue to turn a blind eye.

After that Pretty tried to avoid the chilli-hot whispers and pointing fingers, but by the time she made it to high school her back had been forced down naked by many people she knew in the community. There were always men who wanted to be part of her life, and when they found that they fell short of her expectations they came with currency, and for a poor girl the currency was what mattered.

Then Bongani came along, when she was sweet sixteen. She didn't even want to get to know him – there was nothing about him that interested her – but eventually his father's money engulfed her and swept her off her feet.

Although she felt nothing for him, Bongani worshipped her. He even took her home and introduced her to his parents.

Bongani's mother loved Pretty, and there would have been an engagement and a marriage if Bongani's father hadn't called his son to one side. "Son," he said. "It is a good thing to have a wife. We all love your girlfriend, and are very proud of her, but you and your girlfriend don't yet have the willpower to sit on the red-hot fire that is life. If your mother, son, ever had an affair, that would be the end of us as a family, but although there are many men who want your mother, they know what a strong woman she is. She has resisted them because she has the power to resist, and that is a quality that your girlfriend has not acquired yet. A woman without resistance cannot build a family. Wait, son, and eat it knowing what it is. Don't be surprised later."

Then there was a row in the family because Bongani's mother was pushing for them to get married and his father was resisting. Some members of the family even thought that Bongani's father hated Pretty for some reason, but his father, seeing what was happening, called a meeting. "We all love Pretty," he said, "but I want to ask that they wait until they have both passed their matric. Then, if they still want to, they can marry and we can send them to university together, if they want to go."

Pretty heard about the meeting and knew that after matriculation she would marry into one of the most affluent families in the community, and that she and Bongani would go to university together – if they wanted to. The thought made her smile.

A year later Bongani came to his father with tears in his eyes. He looked like he had just walked a thousand kilometres. "Son, stop crying," his father said, hugging him. "Women are just like that. If you give them your heart they will always find a way to tear it apart."

"She has not acquired the power to resist, Dad," Bongani responded, his voice drenched in tears.

"She will grow up," his father said, trying to comfort his son. "And maybe, when she has grown up, you will still have the power to look her in the eye and love her despite what she has done to you."

But deep down they both knew that Bongani would never forgive her.

When Pretty split with Bongani she was doing Standard Nine and dreaming of becoming a lawyer and defending the defenceless. But after matriculating her dreams were put on hold for two whole years, while she listened to her father's promises. "I am going to take you to the University of the North," he told her. Which became, "I didn't save enough, but let me talk to people . . ." at the beginning of the following year.

Pretty got a job in a supermarket. She didn't like it, but she thought that if she worked there for a year or two she would save enough money to take herself to university. That thought gave her the strength to wake up every morning and go to work, but saving money was more difficult than she had thought it would be, and she soon discovered that the way she was living didn't allow her to save.

One afternoon, when she was working, Sport came to the outlet because he had heard some people talking of her beauty. He had asked that they show him what they were talking about, but they had refused. "There is no need for that," one of them told him. "Just go in there and walk around, if she is on duty you won't miss her."

Sure enough he didn't miss her, and for the first time in his life Sport did not know how to conduct himself in front of a woman.

It was later, during her lunch break, that he approached her. She was window-shopping, unaware that Sport was following her in his sports car, a GT. I have seen beautiful women, but none have scared me as this little girl does, he said to himself, shaking his head.

When Pretty went into a shop, Sport parked his car and followed her. Inside he greeted her humbly: "Hello."

She acknowledged him with a gesture.

"My boss sent me to tell you that you can have anything you want."

"And where is your boss?" she responded, smiling.

"You will see him. He is waiting outside."

"I don't want anything, I am just looking," she replied. "Tell your boss that I said 'thank you'."

"Then I say, on his behalf, that you can take anything you want, anything you want even if you don't want it . . . Take it for your cousins."

Slowly he persuaded her, and eventually he bought her a very expensive pair of shoes, a leather jacket, a pair of jeans, a shirt and some cologne.

They were laughing when they left the shop. "I was instructed to drive you home safely," he said.

"By your boss, I guess," Pretty said.

"You guessed right."

And that was how Sport bought his way into Pretty's heart.

There was nothing wrong with Sport. He seemed to be a sweet man who liked the finer things in life. Pretty never asked how he earned his money, she just accepted whatever he presented of himself, but Sport asked her all about her life and it puzzled him that she never asked about his. "I have asked you nearly everything about your life," he said one day when they were together, "but you have never asked me anything about mine."

"I think it is a good thing not to know too much," Pretty said. "I just accept things as they are, at face value. Don't you think that's for the best?"

"No."

"Well, I think that it is. Ignorance, as they say, is bliss. This way, at ̶ I don't know that I'm being lied to."

"You didn't lie to me, did you?"

"No, but there are questions that I would advise you not to ask."

But after using and abusing her for a couple of months, Sport found himself unable to do anything without having her by his side. "Where is your boyfriend?" he eventually asked.

"Finally," she said, smiling at him. "Finally you ask 'the question'. But, now, I don't know whether to lie to you or tell you the truth. Which do you want me to do?"

"Lie."

"I don't have a boyfriend."

"And what am I?"

"You said lie, and I lied."

Sport looked into the distance as if he was calculating something. "The truth then, Pretty," he finally said. "Where is your boyfriend?"

"You mean my boyfriends."

The answer didn't surprise him; somehow he had always known that she had more than one, but the honesty of her answer made him love her more than ever.

"How many do you have?" he asked.

"I have lost count; they come, they go." She smiled. "But do you really want to know?" she asked, the tone of her voice changing. "Do you really want to know? I don't want to lie to you, so if you don't want to know, please don't ask."

"Do you love your boyfriends?" he asked.

"I have sex with them, if that is where you are going with this." She smiled and gave a laugh that aroused his soul. "But why are you so interested in my private life today? Because, let me tell you, Sport, I don't like to reflect on what I am. I don't like what I am. It is not what I want to be."

While she had been speaking she had changed; her eyes had turned red and her voice had become angry. "You can use me as you want," she continued, "but please don't stir me up." She stopped as tears filled her eyes. "Don't touch my heart."

"I wasn't stirring," Sport protested. "I just wanted to understand why a beautiful, intelligent girl is stuck like you are."

By now the tears were flowing out of her eyes, and she opened the door to get out of the car. "Bitch, what do you think you are doing?" he said, intending to scare her, but immediately he felt ashamed.

"Yes, say that again," she said, stopping to look at him, half in and half out of the car. "Say it again. Say it. Use me like all the other bitches you have used. Don't come here pretending that you want anything more than what you really want. And don't blame me when I give it to you." Her voice, though calm, held a violence that scared him.

They looked at each for a moment, then she wiped away her tears. "You are not the first one to buy me expensive shoes," she said. "You are not the first one to buy me cologne. Men have bought me things all my life, and you know what the funny thing is? I have never asked them for anything. No. They just buy me things, like you did. They just do it." She paused to catch her breath. "You all make up stories," she continued. "'My boss this . . .', 'My boss that . . .' I always say 'no', but they buy me things anyway, just like you did. And, somehow, I have learned to love the fact that they buy me things, because deep down I know that they don't care. After they ejaculate they will move on to someone else, and there will be somebody else for me too. I don't like it, but I didn't choose it either."

"Is that what you think of me?" Sport asked.

"That is what I know about men," she replied, "and you are a man as I am a woman."

38

"Pretty, I want to help you."

"You are stirring me up! Please stop."

"Listen to me . . ."

There were people who had stirred her up before and none of them had ever honoured their promises, but Sport was different, and a few months later Pretty found herself at the University of the North, all her hopes and dreams on fire, the goalposts just three more years away.

Sport was so committed to Pretty that, for once in his life, he focused only on her. He had always had lots of girlfriends, but with Pretty he had found everything he was looking for. He did not need to be with another woman. But Pretty was pretty and it wasn't long before she had a fellowship of wannabe boyfriends, and eventually one of them began to share the stage with Sport. Inevitably, one Tuesday night when they were busy in bed, Pretty heard Sport's GT roaring outside, but she dismissed the idea because Sport only ever visited on weekends – saying that he didn't want to interfere with her studies. But then there was a knock on the door, and the knock was Sport's.

"Who is it?" she asked, and immediately he knew something was wrong because she had never asked him to identify himself before.

Sport knew that the room had burglar bars on the outside, so he relaxed and waited to see what would happen. Finally, after what seemed an eternity, Pretty opened the door. Behind her the boyfriend was sitting on a chair, his books open and a pencil in his hands, trembling a little.

The truth was obvious, but Sport didn't want to believe it. He pushed past Pretty and offered his hand to the boyfriend, watching as the pencil slipped and fell. Sport picked it up, trying to catch the boy's eye as he gave it back to him, but his eyes were running all over the room.

"Don't you think that study time is up?" Sport eventually asked.

The boy didn't know what to say.

"I mean that you can go now," Sport continued. "You can continue studying tomorrow . . ."

Then, finally, the boy offered Sport his hand and they shook hands very hard.

After the boy had left Sport turned to Pretty, took a deep breath and exhaled slowly, trying to compose himself. Even though he had been half expecting it, the fact that she had another boyfriend had hit him hard. He didn't know what to do.

Pretty had talked herself out of almost every situation with men, but this time she didn't know where to start. "I am sorry," she finally said, but it was as if he didn't even hear her. "Sport, I am sorry," she said again, trying to break his silence.

Finally, Sport looked at her, but it was too much for him and he made for the door.

"Sport, don't leave me," she cried.

He paused at the door and wiped away his tears. It was the first time in his life a woman had ever made him cry.

"Sport, I am sorry," she said once more, as he opened the door.

"For what?" he asked violently, closing the door and turning back to her. "What are you sorry for?"

In his line of business you were only sorry when you got caught; sorry because you got caught, but not sorry for the act itself.

"Sport, I am sorry," she repeated, trembling with emotion.

"You're sorry. Yes, Pretty, I understand. But what is it that you are so sorry for?" He took a step towards her and she tripped on the corner of the bed, anticipating the fist that she knew was coming.

"For the last time, Pretty," he said, looking down at her, "what are you sorry for?"

Then he thrashed her, and by the time the campus security came to rescue her there was nothing pretty about her.

*  *  *

The morning after Sport had caught her with her boyfriend, Pretty sat down to think about her prospects. Her father's money had finally come through, but it wasn't even enough to keep her going for a month, and the student fund was only available for the next study year. The truth of it was that without Sport's financial support she would have to abort her studies. It was either that or go begging to him, and she was determined not to do that. She had never begged a man in her whole life. If there was any begging to be done, she was always the one to be begged.

She sat on the single bed, her back to the wall, hugging her legs for comfort, thinking about Bongani and what could have been. Then she began to think about all the other men that she had got naked with, wondering if one of them could help her. She fought the thought, but it wouldn't go away. Just ask, this once, something inside of her said. They are the ones that came to you. They got what they wanted. Ask and get what you want too.

She had never been inclined that way; men were always the ones to come to her with offers, but she had to ask this time. She made a list of all the men that she had got naked with, then separated them into three categories: Grade A, Grade B and Grade C.

Grade A men were those who were family men with financial power. Herbert was the first on the list. She called him at his bottlestore and caught him first time. After they had greeted each other she put forward the purpose of her call: "Well, I am sorry to call you, Herbert, but I have some difficulties with my studies, financial difficulties, and I don't have anywhere else to go. I just thought that maybe you could help me some-how."

"I will call you back," he said, after she had given him the residence phone number, but then he cut the call without even saying goodbye.

Immediately, Pretty felt worse than she had ever felt before in her life and she took to her bed.

Herbert called her the next morning. "How much do you want?" he asked.

She wasn't sure how to respond to the question, so she stayed quiet, calculating.

"Pretty, I said how much do you want?"

Then she told him how much she owed the institution and he gave her all of it, plus fifty per cent.

After Herbert, Pretty tried the next man on the list and then the next. Almost all the men put something towards her education, and that was how she put herself through the University of the North. They had used her, and she was using them in turn.

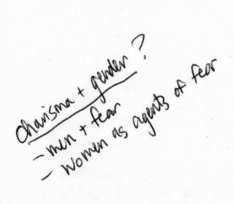
Charisma + gender?
- men + fear
- women as agents of fear

## 7

Khutso loved Pretty from the very first moment he saw her in the lecture hall. She was everything that he wanted in a woman – she disturbed the heat of the sun with her beauty, but she was also superintelligent. However, when he put himself on a virtual weighbridge and judged himself, he realised that she was out of his league. If only I had money like Leruo, I would marry her, he thought to himself.

From that day on he looked for her in every lecture he attended, and as soon as he saw her he would give her a virtual hug and a kiss on her cheek. Sweetheart, how are you? he would ask her in his mind.

I am very well, she would seem to reply.

But if she was not in the lecture hall, and the sun went down without Khutso having laid eyes on her, he would be in torment. He wouldn't be able to study and would be back in his room before half past nine.

One evening, Tshepo saw the worry on his face for the umpteenth time. "That little girl is not eating you again, is she?" he asked.

"I can't study," Khutso said.

"Khutso, I told you to face the woman and pour your heart out," Tshepo told his friend. "And now I am telling you again. You will feel relieved, because either she will tell you to fuck off or she will hug you. I would prefer that she told you to fuck off because, honestly, if a woman of that calibre ever hugged me I would go crazy. And look at you . . . You are already crazy and you haven't even talked to her."

But Tshepo's words didn't help, and, unable to sleep, Khutso decided to take a walk. Purposeless, his feet dragged him through the beautiful, moonless night in the direction of her residence. Once inside, he walked past her room twice, staring at the door as if, if he stared hard enough, he might be able to see through it. A few minutes later he found himself outside again, looking up at the light coming from her window. In his mind he asked her, Sweetheart, is there anything wrong, are you all right?

He stood there, as if waiting for her to respond. After some time he saw a shadow on the curtain and it seemed to him, from the way it moved, that she was dancing to a favourite tune. He did not even think that maybe the shadow belonged to her roommate, to him it was Pretty's shadow, and she seemed to say, I am all right. You can go now and have a sweet sleep, my dear. Then she blew him a kiss.

Khutso smiled, accepting the kiss, knowing that he would be able to rest now that he had seen her. Then he turned and walked back to his room, his heart satisfied.

* * *

And so their first year went by, with Khutso silently enduring the self-tormenting love he had for Pretty – though Tshepo often encouraged him to explain himself to her, he never said anything.

In the second year they bumped into each other outside the library. "Oh! Sorry, very sorry, Khutso," she said, looking at him.

He stood stock-still as she walked away. He wanted to say, "I am sorry too. Yes, Khutso is my name and you are Pretty. Hello." But the words wouldn't come out. The fact that she knew his name had taken him completely by surprise.

"She knows my name," he bragged to Tshepo. "She really knows my name."

Tshepo tried to make him see that she was bound to know his name because they had shared the lecture hall every week for a year, but Khutso believed what he needed to believe.

Finally, halfway through their third year, Khutso and Pretty started talking. Pretty had known that he had been watching her from a distance for a long time and had labelled him a patient admirer. At the start of the third year she greeted him a couple of times, just to see if a conversation would develop, but he would only raise his hand to acknowledge her. She knew that she had rendered him speechless, but she enjoyed the fact that he didn't approach her, trying to buy her this or that, trying to talk her into this or that.

For Khutso the fact that she would say "hi" to him every now and then was overwhelming, and after each and every time he was tormented by his thoughts: She likes me. She wants me. She is just being friendly. She is just . . . But he always ended up at the same thought: There is nothing about me she could possibly like.

Then one afternoon, after they had attended a late-afternoon lecture, she invited him for supper. Immediately, Khutso forgot everything that he had planned to do that evening. The idea of the appointment filled him with an awful anxiety, and by the time he got back to his room he was sweating.

"Khutso, what's going on?" Tshepo asked, looking at his friend. "Look at you."

"What do you think she wants?" he asked his roommate after he had explained the situation. "Do you think that she loves me?"

"Look at yourself," Tshepo said. "I told you that that woman would drive you crazy."

"You think I am going crazy?" Khutso asked. "I don't know, but I think I feel like this because I love her."

"It is better to keep that kind of woman on the wall," Tshepo said, pointing at the posters of naked white women on his side of the room. "They are for relieving the pressures of life, for fuelling dreams, but you, my friend, are going to have supper with one."

Tshepo looked at Khutso, but he wasn't listening to him, he was in a world of his own. "How are you going to kiss her and remain sane?" he asked Khutso. "I think you . . ."

"Pretty . . ." Khutso said, interrupting him. "Pretty, what are you doing to me?"

Tshepo waved his hand in front of his roommate's face, but he was deep in his own thoughts. "And I thought that you said that you had experience with women," he said, picking his bag up from the bed and leaving Khutso to his thoughts.

For the next two hours Khutso tried to titivate himself. Finally, at five minutes to eight, he got up from his bed and walked over to the door, but when he got there he found that he couldn't leave the room. Walking around the room, he tried to calm himself down, but he couldn't help his mind filling with questions: What was she going to say to him? Why had she invited him to supper? What was he going to say to her?

Eventually, all the other lights in the residence went out and all he could see was darkness, and it was then that he knew he had stood her up.

* * *

When Pretty saw Khutso the following Monday, she walked straight up to him. She wasn't offended, as he had thought she would be, and she didn't ask what had happened either. If he had seen her first, he would have tried to hide, but it was she who saw him.

"People always hug each other, but I have never hugged you," she said as she embraced him warmly. And it was then that Pretty and Khutso started talking properly.

A few days later Pretty woke up with Khutso in her bed. She looked at him, thinking that he was the most beautiful man she had ever slept with. Since Bongani she had never thought of marriage, but that morning the thought just came into her head and she wished that he would say the big words. Yes, he is poor, she thought to herself, but he is going to get a degree, and we . . . She smiled at the thought of "we". We will be fine.

Khutso turned over, made waking-up noises and began to stretch his muscles, his usual waking-up routine, but then the thought of Pretty popped into his mind and he opened his eyes quickly. They looked at each other and then he smiled.

"Good morning," she said and smiled back at him.

But he did not respond.

"Good morning, sweetheart," she said, trying again.

"Morning," he finally said, his voice unsure.

She pulled him close and he held her tightly. "I always wondered why God created a man and a woman, because men and women are always fighting," she said. "They are always in constant conflict with each other. But maybe He, God, created us for moments like this, when we are together, truly together as we are now . . ." She stopped, looking at him, then smiled. "Yes, I want to get married, I do. I really do want to get married, and I want you not only to be my husband but to be my best friend. I have lived a troubled life and I want it to end. Khutso, I want to start afresh with you."

She continued talking and talking and it seemed to Khutso as if her words had been taken out of his own mouth; words like "husband", "we" and "our" shocked and excited him. He had always thought that

47

the first girl he made love to would be the woman that he would marry. He had always wondered why men wanted to bed everything that had breasts; it seemed such a waste of time and energy.

Khutso looked at Pretty and smiled. What am I doing with you? he wondered. What on earth did I do to deserve to be with you?

"Because you love me," she answered him, as if she had read his thoughts. "You love me, but not just because you want to use me."

Her eyes started to fill with tears. "In my life I never had that many people who loved me," she said. "All the men who said they loved me just wanted to see me naked, and after they had used me a few times they all moved on. But you love me and I just want you to love me. I love you. I am yours. All yours."

Khutso could not bear to look into her tearful eyes. He did not know what to say. Her past didn't matter to him, but the fact that she had told him that she loved him had left him speechless.

"I love you too," he finally said. "I loved you from the first day I saw you in the lecture hall."

"I have done things that I am ashamed of," Pretty began, "but I can't erase them, so I hope that you can live with them." She paused. "You see, Khutso, I am a poor girl," she said, sounding as if she were praying for mercy. "My mother passed away when I was seven years old."

And with that she laid bare her past.

"You are not talking," she said when she had finished her story. "Are you scared?"

"No, not at all," he replied. "I just don't think that you should be ashamed of your past." Everybody has a past, he thought to himself, and how could a girl like her – with her family background – not have a past like she has.

"I am not some little rich girl. I had to make hard choices," she con-

48

tinued, "but I love you, Khutso, and I would like you to understand what I am, so that you can help me start over again."

* * *

Khutso didn't sleep well that night. Even though Pretty's past didn't bother him, his dreams took him to the sea and he found that he couldn't stand against it; the waves pulled him off his feet.

The following night, Pretty invited him to supper. After they had eaten, they sat in her room and talked. "Tell me about your girlfriends," she suddenly asked.

"I don't have a girlfriend," Khutso replied, the answer jumping out of his mouth because it was true. "I've never had one."

"Do you mean that I am your first-ever girlfriend?"

"Yes, you are . . ."

She giggled. "You mean that you have never slept with a woman in all your life?" she asked.

He nodded, even though it was a lie – the truth was too shameful to admit.

"I want you to sleep here with me tonight," she declared.

And with that he felt as if he was suddenly on dry land; his two feet firmly on the ground.

# 8

Everything was perfect. Khutso had the girl that he had always wanted, and when he walked down the street with Pretty all eyes turned his way: male eyes that said "You are a lucky bastard!" and female eyes that asked "Why can't I be like her?".

One day, when he and Tshepo were walking on campus together, Tshepo looked at him and smiled. "Excuse my language," he said. "But now, my friend and soon-to-be former roommate, now you can fuck any woman you want."

"Why do you say that?" Khutso asked.

"Women have an inferiority complex. They see you with Marilyn Monroe and they all want to get naked with you. *You*, my former roommate. There is no better time than now. We sacrificed ourselves in high school, turned a blind eye as students, but now it is time to engage on full power. We have to fuck 'em all . . ."

"No, Tshepo," Khutso said, shaking his head. "I've got all that I need in Pretty."

"I am not saying end that relationship," Tshepo continued. "How can I ask you to leave Marilyn Monroe? No, all I am saying is let's do some damage on the side."

Tshepo was on a raid – a careless raid – and twelve months after graduating he had five children with five different women, and that was just the beginning.

*  *  *

The first time Khutso's mother ever saw Pretty was during the holidays at the end of his final year. He had been home from university for eleven days, relaxing and enjoying the fact that he was sure to have passed all his exams with flying colours.

The university had completed his alienation from his community and since he had been back home he had spent most of his days indoors reading newspapers and his favourite novels.

"If education makes people this unsociable then this education should be banned," his mother told him. "You can't spend your days reading. You have an education. Now, son, you have to get yourself a wife and friends, and you can't find a wife or friends in the newspaper." But Khutso knew that deep down she was really happy.

Pretty showed up at their gate that afternoon. Khutso's mother saw the car and thought that it had come to deliver her monthly groceries, but, instead, a pretty young woman got out, and the car reversed back in the direction it had come from.

The four thin dogs that barked at everything that came into their yard stood up, their eyes fixed on the young woman as she made her way up to the makeshift gate. She opened it slowly, unsure of her safety, but the dogs just observed her as she closed the gate behind her and made her way towards the house.

Khutso's mother looked at Pretty in the same way as her dogs, and their nosey neighbours also stopped whatever it was that they were doing, but Pretty was used to eyes watching her every move and she walked on.

Then Khutso's mother told Pretty their surname, and asked if she was sure that she was in the right place.

"Yes," Pretty replied. "I am a friend of Khutso's."

The old woman stopped as if she had just been hit by a bullet. The hoe slid slowly from her hand and fell to the ground, then she jumped

51

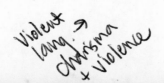
Violent lang. → charisma + violence

up ululating, reciting the family's praise poem and Khutso's praise poem. And all her seven live-in grandchildren came out to see what was going on in the yard.

The noise also woke the napping Khutso, but when he saw Pretty standing outside, surrounded by his nephews and nieces, he felt scared. He hadn't believed Pretty when she had told him that she would come over to his place in the holidays, and now he didn't know what he was going to do about her. Where was she going to sleep? What was she going to eat?

Meanwhile, outside, Khutso's mother had paused in her celebrations. "Are you sure you aren't lost?" she asked Pretty again, just to confirm.

"No," Pretty replied. "I am sure that I am at the right place."

Khutso's mother looked at her, then at her grandchildren, then back at Pretty. "Makoti, do you eat goat meat?" she finally asked.

"Yes, I do," Pretty said, looking a little puzzled but smiling all the same. "I like it very much. It is the gods' preferred meat."

Khutso's mother looked at the goat barn. "Go, take Kokwane," she commanded the eldest of her grandchildren – Kokwane was the oldest female goat in the herd, and although she didn't know it yet, she had just had her last afternoon.

"I am sorry, but a goat is all I have," Khutso's mother said to Pretty, taking her bag from her and leading her onto the stoep. "Eat it because I am giving it with all my heart."

Khutso's mother then took out a new blanket and put it down on the stoep. She asked Pretty to sit on the new blanket and then she sat down on the mud floor and greeted her formally.

After the goat was done, Khutso's mother took the liver and asked Pretty to salt and cook it. Then everybody was invited to come and enjoy the goat liver that had been cooked by Khutso's wife-to-be.

There had been times when his mother had been worried about Khutso's lack of interest in girls. She had even, at times, thought that he might be a homosexual, but Pretty's appearance eased her mind.

Pretty stayed for five days and quickly became the darling of the community. A few days after she had left, his mother came into Khutso's bedroom. "Your wife, she is beautiful," she said.

"Ma, I am not married."

"Your girlfriend, she is beautiful."

Khutso was quiet, waiting for his mother to say whatever it was she had come to say to him.

"But you know her better than we do," she continued. "We have only seen what she wanted us to see. How much of that beauty goes inside, only you know." She laughed. "Your father said that men only marry because it is a vital part that a man must have a wife and not because they want to." She smiled, thinking that when those words were uttered they hurt her, and now she saw some truth within them and she forgave him. How foolish of me, she thought. "If I were a man –"

"Ma," Khutso said, interrupting her, "you are not a man and you can never be."

"Yes. But I am a woman and you are going to marry a woman just like me."

"She is not anything like you. She has a degree."

"Education." She smiled proudly. "You can be educated," she said, "but you are still my child."

She thought how sad it was that women never had a peacefully perfect relationship with their sons, but they raise them, and this was the foundation of why women can never have a peacefully perfect relationship with their men.

*   *   *

1986 was a year like no other. When it began Khutso and Pretty were head over heals in love, working as interns – serving articles. They hadn't yet got to the self-promised land but the road was clear. The destination was in sight, and only time separated them from it.

By June of 1987, Khutso had managed to pay for the completion of his mother's house, and it became the seventh house in the village to have electricity. Pretty, meanwhile, had built her father a two-roomed house alongside the three mud huts that she had grown up in. Then, as the people were celebrating the initiation of the young boys into manhood, a delegation from Khutso's family met with representatives from Pretty's family.

Many years earlier, before Pretty had been born, her maternal family had come to declare her mother's pregnancy to her paternal family. Then her father had been called to come and answer for himself. "Do you know this girl?" her grandfather's brother had asked her father, pointing at Pretty's mother.

The question was ambiguous, the real question was: Did you get this young girl pregnant?

Pretty's father looked down at the ground, a sure sign of a guilty soul. "No," he had said, "I don't know her." He had not wanted to show disrespect to the old people by admitting to such an act in front of them.

But Pretty's paternal grandmother would not have it. "Look at her carefully," she'd said to the young man, "because she has put on a lot of weight since I last saw you sneaking her out of your compound! What was she doing there?"

After that he had not been able to deny it any more, and so when Pretty was born her paternal family paid damages to her maternal family: five goats, six chickens and a cock. And though the payment was not lobola, her mother had stayed with her paternal family from that day on.

54

For their daughter, things were different. Delegations from the two families met and followed the traditional protocols for uniting two families. However, they quickly discovered that there wasn't much that Pretty's father wanted – he was just thankful that his daughter had graduated, but was afraid to even ask how the miracle had happened. "A daughter has to marry," he finally said. "What I am asking is that her husband sees to it that her siblings, my daughter and son, go to university, so that they too can graduate with degrees . . ." Tears filled his eyes and he paused to regain composure. "That is the lobola that I demand."

Pretty and Khutso opted to have a white wedding, and what a wedding it became; there was good food and beer, and everyone danced till late morning on Sunday, when the groom and bride finally left for their honeymoon.

* * *

Pretty and Khutso advanced swiftly through the corporate jungle – working hard, changing jobs, going up and up to the financially greener pastures of the homeland.

At the end of 1988 they bought the four-roomed house in Seshego that they had been renting. But Khutso wasn't satisfied; he also wanted to rent out property. So, in 1989, they bought two four-roomed houses that they rented out.

They were happy. Khutso grew dull, except for his array of ties, and nursed a beard and moustache. Early on in their marriage Pretty had tried to make him into a model, but she had failed. His suits were expensive, but if you didn't know you would have thought he wore the same clothes from Monday to Friday. Even on Sundays, when they went to church, he didn't look that different – he was always dressed formally.

In contrast, Pretty had her hair done every weekend and always had a new wardrobe. Khutso didn't mind the expense; he liked the fact that she took such good care of herself and enjoyed every second he was with her. In fact, he loved being with her so much that he tried to stop her learning to drive, and when she did finally pass her driving test, he didn't want her to have her own car. "Honey, we are always together," he said. "We do everything together. We have survived all these years with one car and I love it this way. Besides, getting another car is a waste of money."

In reality, though, this was just an excuse to stop Pretty driving. Although in the years since they had graduated Khutso had learnt to trust Pretty, he still thought that Pretty driving herself would give her too much freedom. By driving her around he always knew where she was, what was she doing and who she was with. And, because he objected, Pretty put the thought of having another car out of her mind.

# 9

Khutso's thought brought a smile to his face. "This is it!" he said out loud.

"What?" Pretty asked.

"We have reached the place. This is it."

"This is it?" she asked, smiling as she looked around.

"Indeed it is."

"This is it . . ." Pretty repeated, finally understanding his meaning.

They hugged, not able to find the words to describe "it" or the hard journey it had taken to reach "it" but feeling fulfilled nonetheless. They were both the first from their families to graduate and achieve success in the corporate world, and Khutso thought that his mother would be very happy when he told her that he had finally reached the place where she had always wanted him to be.

"Don't cry," Pretty said, seeing the tears welling up in his eyes.

"I am not crying," Khutso replied.

They looked at each other and he wiped away her tears. "I am not crying," he repeated. "It is just that we are here."

Then Khutso kissed her and seconds later, caught up in the moment, they were at it.

"Khu," she said when they finally got to the finish line, out of breath and lying naked on the hard floor. "I should have had my period last week."

He looked at her. I am going to be a father, he thought, and the thought brought a smile to his face.

There were times in Pretty's life when she had longed to be pregnant, when she had felt sad because almost all the girls she knew had babies, and they had looked at her like at a barren woman. Because of this her pregnancy became the most important thing that she had ever done; she was never afraid and when it came to it, she showed off her belly with pride.

\* \* \*

1992. Nearly five and a half years after their wedding Thapelo was born, healthy and fat as a bear. The only problem was that his eyes were closed and he could not seem to open them, but the doctors reassured them that he would be all right. By the time he was three weeks old he could open them to the size of a coin slot, and at the start of his second month his eyes were fully open and it was clear that he could see very well.

Then it was time to think of a name for the little boy. Khutso encouraged everyone to come up with a name and in the end there were eighty-four suggestions. The proud parents wrote each name on a playing card, and after the cards had been shuffled Pretty's father – the boy's only living grandfather – picked a card. Then Khutso's mother – his only living grandmother – picked a card. It was Khutso's mother who picked the card with "Thapelo" written on it, but both names were put to vote and Thapelo was the one that won.

Khutso took the little bundle of life and balanced it in his huge hands. How could someone dump this in a dustbin? he wondered to himself. How could someone leave this on another man's doorstep? He couldn't think of a logical explanation. Maybe, if the child were the result of non-consensual sex, a woman might do such a thing, he thought. But the child hadn't raped anyone. Maybe an act like that was the result of extreme levels of poverty. But he had survived extreme poverty. Many people had survived extreme poverty and lived to tell the tale.

Khutso raised Thapelo high above his head, closed his eyes and called on God and the gods to give him and his wife the power to raise their child in a responsible manner. He asked them that should he ever fail, they should protect the child and help him to grow up to be his own man.

* * *

At seven months Thapelo stopped sucking his mother's breast, and two months later he was walking. He never crawled, just pulled himself up, using the coffee table, and began to walk around it.

Three months later it was Thapelo's first birthday. Pretty invited everybody, but because both their families were poor she had to pay for most of them to travel to the party.

"These people aren't even going to bring Thapelo a present," Khutso had protested when he first saw the guest list, thinking of all their hard-earned money going to waste.

"Who cares?" Pretty had replied. "They are Thapelo's relatives; he is important to them and they are important to him. And, yes, they won't bring him any presents. Why?" She paused, looking hard at Khutso. "Because they are poor. That's why," she continued. "But they love him, and that is what they are bringing him . . . their love."

So, in the week leading up to the birthday party, there were people sleeping on the floor in every room of their house, and by Thursday, Thapelo's actual birthday, their bedroom had become a female dormitory; the men were sleeping in the sitting room and kitchen.

Although Thursday had been Thapelo's birthday, Saturday was the day of his party. Khutso had invited Tshepo, his wife and their two children. Pretty had asked him not to invite them – she didn't like who Tshepo had become, and hated to pretend that she liked him – but Khutso couldn't very well leave his best friend off the guest list.

"Boy, boy, boy, you are going to be just like your father: overrighteous and godly," Tshepo said loudly, putting down his can of beer and picking Thapelo up. "I am an African, I have never celebrated my own birthday, and I don't see the purpose of celebrating birthdays, but happy birthday anyway."

Then Tshepo looked back at his unhappy wife – who had resigned herself to living an unhappy life – and his children and smiled.

\* \* \*

Khutso's mother had prepared home-made beer during the week and by Saturday morning it was just right.

Pretty, her father and two uncles, and Khutso, his mother and sisters formed a circle around a flower – the selected connection between the dead and the living. Then they drank and spilt the beer onto the flower, calling their ancestors to come, to bless the house and protect and bless everyone who was living in it.

After the blessing, the party went on until the early hours of the morning. There were lots of people, and Khutso's heart was gladdened by all the people from the township who had come to his house to drink his beer and eat his food. He felt that the township had accepted him.

"Son," Pretty's father said, shaking Khutso by the shoulder, "you are not sleeping, are you?"

Khutso had collapsed in a chair, watching Pretty's uncles as they happily drank the night away. "No, no, no. I am happy," he replied, his eyes closing as his head fell back as if seeking a headrest. "I am very happy."

\* \* \*

60

Horrible. That was how Pretty felt as the tears ran down her cheeks. She was sad beyond words.

Tshepo and his family had been involved in an accident after Thapelo's birthday party. No one had survived the car crash.

The whole family was buried the following Saturday, but Pretty couldn't bring herself to go to the funeral. The words Tshepo had said to her at the party came back to her again and again. "Pretty, do you have life insurance?" he had asked her. "If you don't have any, you should get some. And if you don't get that, then you should get yourself a good sangoma." He had paused to take a sip of beer. "Black people don't like educated people like you and me," he had continued. "And if you die, your children will be left naked. Get yourself some life insurance."

When she finally recovered from the shock of Tshepo's death, Pretty took out four life insurance policies – two for herself and two for Khutso. The monthly payments were costly, but at least every time Tshepo's question floated into her head she could answer it. "I have four," she would say. "Tshepo, I have four."

# 10

Thapelo was his father's pride and joy. There was nothing more important in Khutso's life than his son, and he soon became both Thapelo's
mother and father – washing, dressing and feeding Thapelo before drop-
ping him off at nursery school on his way to work. In fact, so engrossed
in Thapelo's life did Khutso become, that Pretty felt like she had become
a phantom in their house. But she didn't worry too much, she thought
that whatever it was that Khutso had for his son would wear off soon
enough. And anyway, his obsession with their son had finally allowed
her to get the car that she had always wanted – as Khutso couldn't run
around after Thapelo and make sure that she got to her appointments
on time.

"Khutso, I told you I had an important meeting," she had complained
after the third or fourth time he had forgotten her. "I even reminded
you before you left."

"Honey, why don't you get your own car . . ." he had replied, without
even looking up from what he was doing with Thapelo.

So Pretty bought her father's dream car for herself. Her father had
showed it to her years earlier – one afternoon when they were visiting
her mother at the hospital (this was before she had died). Twice her
father had made the young Pretty walk around the car. "Don't touch it,
just look at it," he had told her. "I promise you, my child, your father is
going to work hard and come back home driving this machine of the
Germans. You know, when you are travelling in this car . . ."

Her father had talked and talked about the car that day. Pretty didn't remember his words, but he had been right – her new car was a joyful ride.

*  *  *

On Saturdays Khutso would wake up and look at his son where he lay in bed next to him. Smiling, he would wait for Thapelo to wake up, watching him while he slept. Then father and son would take a long bath together, after which they would prepare breakfast for just the two of them. Once breakfast was over, they were out.

"Can I come with?" Pretty would ask, but she was always told the same thing: "We don't have room for females. Sorry, honey, but this is a man thing, a father-and-son kind of a thing." theme of manhood Then they were gone.

Even though there was a baby's car seat in the back of the car, Thapelo would sit on his father's lap, trying to turn the steering wheel left and right as Khutso drove to wherever it was that he had decided to take his son that particular morning. In fact, Thapelo loved driving so much that when he was three, Khutso let go of the steering wheel when they were in a deserted parking area and let Thapelo steer the car. "Where are you going?" Khutso asked him, stopping the car before it hit a wall. "You could have damaged my car. How can I trust you with my car if you are going to drive like that?"

He put the car in reverse. "Don't turn the steering wheel without looking at where you are going," he told his son.

Back at home – after their drive – Khutso would read stories to Thapelo. He taught him how to count and how to read. He taught him how to write and how to draw.

Finally, when he was four years old, Khutso taught Thapelo how to fight. "You are a man now, you must fight your own wars, son. This life is about fighting," he told him. "I am here for you now, but one day you will have to stand up for yourself."

Thapelo learned never to cry while he was with his father, even if something did cause him a lot of pain. "Daddy, I am hurt," he had said the first time it had happened, trying hard to suppress the pain that he felt.

Khutso had looked at the injury, then he squeezed the skin around it hard. "It is painful?" he asked.

"Yes."

"Sorry, son, but you are growing up," he continued, smiling while the tears ran down Thapelo's cheeks.

"Hey!" Khutso said, pretending to get angry. "Wipe away your tears. You are a man now, and pain is part and parcel of this life. They go together, hand in hand. You should never cry."

And so every time Thapelo hurt himself when Khutso was around he would dust himself down, and if there was blood he would wipe it away, because he knew better than to let his father see that he had hurt himself.

\* \* \*

One day, when Thapelo was five years old, Khutso gave him some money. "Thapelo, you need anything?" he asked. "Here, you buy yourself anything you want."

Khutso loved to watch the amazement on people's faces when they saw a child pushing a trolley around a shop. He would watch from a distance, pretending that he didn't know Thapelo, as his son took all the sweets and chocolates he wanted and put them into the trolley. And when Thapelo went to pay, Khutso would wait for him at the door, his heart bursting with pride as his son paid for his sweets.

Thapelo usually never answered the cashier's questions, he just con-tinued doing what he was doing, but once a whole supermarket came to a standstill, the police were called and it was announced throughout the whole mall that there was a lost child in Pick 'n Pay.

"I'm not lost," Thapelo had said, looking at them and shaking his head.

"Where are you from?" the cashier had asked.

"Home."

"Where is home?"

"Seshego, Zone One."

"And what is your name?"

"Thapelo."

But the police had already been called, and when Khutso went to claim his child, after enjoying the little show, the manager wouldn't let him leave the store until they had arrived.

"Did my son say that he was lost?" Khutso had asked him angrily. "He was just paying for some sweets and chocolates. You people are wasting your own time for nothing."

"You shouldn't let children walk around alone, it is a crime," the manager had replied, his eyes expressing his fury. "It is a crime."

"He was being watched at all times," Khutso had responded, but they still had to wait for the police to settle the dispute.

Then, one afternoon, Thapelo asked Khutso for money as they pulled into a filling station. "Dad, I want a drink," he commanded.

Khutso looked at him.

"Dad, can I please have something to drink, please," he said, rephras-ing his request.

Khutso gave him a fifty-rand note and asked him to get him a news-paper as well.

A few minutes later Thapelo came back with his father's much-loved Sunday newspaper, but Khutso noticed immediately that the change was short.

Thapelo had never really cared about change – he just took whatever the cashiers gave him – and he was frightened by his father's reaction. Seeing this, Khutso introduced his son to the mathematics of money. He changed a fifty-rand note into coins and notes. "Let us say, son, that you are a businessman and I am a customer. I want to buy something that costs five rand, but I give you ten rand; how much change should you give me back?"

Khutso started out simply, but he made the game harder every time. Thapelo loved it. They called it the customer and the businessman, and they played it every weekend.

*   *   *

Khutso gave Thapelo so much confidence that he believed that he could do anything. This wasn't a problem when Khutso was around, but when Thapelo was left with his nanny he wanted to do everything his father had taught him. In the morning, he would climb on a chair so he could switch on the stove, pour oil into a pan and put it on the heat. Then he would take that same chair to the fridge and take out the eggs and bacon. But Thapelo's nannies weren't like his father, and they would try to stop him cooking breakfast. "She doesn't love me, Daddy, and I don't love her," he would tell his father every time his nanny stopped him from doing something, and after that it usually wasn't long before the nanny left.

Thapelo didn't like his mother very much either, and when he was with her they often fought. "Mummy, I don't love you any more," he would say. "You are not my mummy any more."

So, although Khutso was a hard father, Thapelo preferred his company to that of his mother, and it was in this way that he took their togetherness away from his parents. He divided Khutso and Pretty. He even settled his father's concerns about his mother's whereabouts: What was she doing? Who was she with? And what time would she be home? Khutso, it seemed, no longer cared. If Pretty wasn't home when they came back from wherever they had been, he and Thapelo would go out again, to the movies, and come back much later in the evening.

So it was that Khutso and Pretty became two people who merely shared a bed.

\* \* \*

One particular Saturday Thapelo and Khutso came home late. Pretty had waited for them until nine, but when they hadn't been home by half past she had decided to go out. However, it didn't worry Thapelo and his father that she wasn't home, and when Pretty finally did return, early in the morning, Khutso didn't ask where she had been. In fact, he didn't say anything to her until she confronted him.

"What am I in this family?" she asked him angrily. "Where do I fit in with this father-and-son thing? Every time it's 'Honey, it's a male thing . . .', 'Honey, it's a father-and-son thing . . .'. Where do I fit in?"

Khutso watched as tears filled her eyes.

"I don't feel like a mother in this family," she continued. "Everything is always about you two. I am not part of your lives. I am not part of anything. I feel like a ghost in this house."

"Pre," he said, embracing her, trying to calm her down, "I am not a perfect man."

"Who is perfect, Khutso?" she asked as they looked deep into each other's eyes. "I don't want you to be perfect, but these days everything

67

revolves around Thapelo. And if you are not with Thapelo you are at work, and I only get a kiss 'good morning', 'goodbye' and 'goodnight'." She paused. "All I want is to be part of your life, not an afterthought."

"But, Pre, I love you," he said.

"You don't love me," she replied, the river of tears bursting its banks. "You have stopped loving me. You used to love me: I felt it; you were concerned; you cared. But you are not that Khutso any more."

"Pretty, I am sorry," he said.

Pretty thought that maybe Khutso just needed to be made a little jealous, so a week or so later she sent herself some e-mails and then asked him to check her mail for her. Khutso did check her e-mail – after she had asked for the fourth time – but unfortunately he just opened the e-mails and printed them out, without even reading the contents.

The next day Thapelo's nanny told Khutso, "Your wife is lonely."

Khutso didn't know what to say to her. He had spoken with her before, but it was the first time in the four years that they had had a nanny working for them that any one of the women had said something to him about his personal life.

"Son, it is not good for a woman to be alone in a marriage," the nanny continued. "It is not healthy for the marriage and the family." Then she got on with her work.

That afternoon Khutso sent Pretty flowers at work and bought her a present, a diamond necklace. When she got home he kissed her and they went out to dinner, just the two of them. "Pretty, I love you and, most importantly, I want you," he told her as they sat opposite one another in the restaurant, but as he said the words he realised that he was thinking of the words of a certain song: "Said I told you that I love you and there ain't no more to say."

"Let's dance to our song," he said to stop himself talking.

"Ask them to play it first."

"I will sing it for you."

Then they were on their feet – cheek to cheek – as if they were dancing to a song that was playing, while Khutso sang, whispering their song to her: "Nomakanjani we dali wam . . ."

"Are you happy?" Khutso asked her when they sat down again at the table.

"Do I look happy?" she asked him.

"No. Why aren't you happy?"

"Because I have a view of how a family should be, and my view and the way this family is are not the same."

"Pretty, I am sorry," Khutso said again.

But that was his problem, his remorse was the remorse of the moment, and although he felt bad he couldn't change his ways.

There were many instances in the months that followed that evening when Pretty tried to show Khutso what was happening to their marriage. He never denied any of it, but after they had had a talk and he had cried – because he did cry every time she showed him the potholes in his marriage – he would always default to his old ways.

# 11

At the start of 2002 Thapelo began Grade Four at Mitchell House Preparatory School. He was turning ten later in the year. It was his first big birthday and Khutso wanted Thapelo to celebrate it with his friends from school, but as with his first birthday, his mother wanted it to be a big family affair. "I want to celebrate my son's life with his family," she told Khutso.

"That's an excuse."

"Yes, I know, Khutso," Pretty said. "I am making an excuse to celebrate my son's life. You grew up without celebrating birthdays. I totally understand. You and your people like to celebrate people when they are dead. You like to talk well of them when they can't hear a word, and spare no expense for their funeral, treating them like they are gods. Why not celebrate a living soul instead?"

Khutso looked at her; she sounded strange. "Honey –" he began.

"Khutso, I am not in the mood," she said, interrupting him. "Go play with your son and leave me alone."

And then, for the first time in their life together, she walked out on him.

In a repeat of Thapelo's first birthday, Pretty invited everyone from both sides of the family, and some of them, like Khutso's mother, came and stayed in their house for three weeks before the party. Once again, Khutso was not impressed. "These people aren't even going to bring Thapelo a present," he said, repeating what he had said nine years earlier.

"You said that the last time," Pretty replied, tears suddenly filling her eyes. "And, yes, you were right, they didn't bring him presents. But this is not about presents, it is about celebrating my baby's life with his family. They don't have much, but they still care about him."

Khutso was puzzled. He wanted to ask her why she was crying, but he couldn't find the words, so instead he kept quiet and when she brought him a bill to pay he paid it.

\* \* \*

Thapelo blew out the ten candles on his cake with one breath.

"Make a wish!" everyone yelled at him.

"I wish to have a birthday party every Saturday," he said, and they all laughed and sang "Happy Birthday" to him.

It was a happy day. Most of the guests had come with their parents, so there were really two parties going on at the same time: Thapelo's birthday party, with his friends by the pool, and the other party where his adult guests were celebrating Thapelo's day in their adult way.

At one point everybody was called together and Pretty's uncle made a short speech and asked anybody who had something to say to say it. Then he gave Thapelo's parents a chance to speak.

"I never had a birthday," Khutso said, and everybody laughed. "When I was young I attended many birthday parties," he continued, "but I never had one of my own. I always thought it was because my father wasn't alive, but when I asked my mother about it, she explained to me that even though she had never had a party for me she celebrated my birthday each and every day of her life. From then on I knew that my birthday was each and every day, and that it was better than everyone else's birthday that only came once a year. And that is what I do every day of my life, son. I celebrate your birth. I am celebrating your life every day of my life."

Thapelo was asked to make the final speech. He thanked everybody who had come to his party, especially his friends. "Dad," he concluded, "I, too, celebrate your life each and every day."

Pretty looked at her child, tears filling her eyes as she bit her lip. Then she called him to her, gave him a warm hug and picked him up as they all sung "Happy Birthday" to him once again.

* * *

Late that night, when Thapelo was in bed, Pretty came into his room. "Thapelo," she said, sitting down on the edge of his bed.

He looked at her, but he was too tired to do anything other than smile.

"Thapelo, Mother is dying and you will soon be left all alone," Pretty continued. "Daddy is going to hang around with you for some time, but I think that he is dying too. Be a strong boy. Enjoy your life to the fullest because we are all dying."

But Thapelo hadn't heard a word. He had fallen asleep.

* * *

"Honey, what do you think counts as a fulfilled life?" Pretty asked her husband. "Do you think that if I passed away people would say that I had lived a fulfilled life?"

Khutso looked at her and smiled. "Don't think about dying," he said, moving closer and hugging her. "Think about living."

The weeks before Thapelo's tenth birthday had been the most difficult of their marriage because they had had to pretend to their family that all was well between them, but at that moment, when Khutso looked at Pretty, it seemed to him that the party had fixed everything. "I love you," he said.

"You love Thapelo," she replied, tears filling her eyes.

72

Then they were at it, but her heart wasn't in it, she didn't really want to. Then, suddenly, she became angry. It was as if she wanted to tear Khutso apart. It was as if she was fighting him or punishing him for something.

*   *   *

Pretty had taken countless tests, and she had never been scared that the result might be positive, but she still always asked for the pre-counselling. On the day she had taken her last test, the counsellor had looked at her strangely. "You don't look scared," she'd said.

"I have taken the test a couple of times before," Pretty admitted. "But I still want the counselling."

And so she listened to the pre-counselling one more time.

After the test results, she had looked at the report and smiled. Then she sat through the post-counselling with the same smile stuck on her face. But on the way home the tears began to flow, and then she started to cry so hard that she had to stop the car on the side of the road.

Two hours later she had run out of tears. Her mind exhausted, she had decided to drive under the trailer of a truck. She drove and drove, looking for a truck, but the next thing she saw was Khutso opening the garage door for her.

*   *   *

One afternoon, a few days after Thapelo's birthday, someone at work found Pretty collapsed in her office chair. She was rushed to hospital, but was pronounced dead on arrival. The doctor wrote *chemically induced death* on the death certificate.

Khutso was distraught at losing Pretty. He had never realised how much he needed her until she was no longer by his side, and he blamed himself for her death. He knew he hadn't been the greatest husband, and he wished that she would come back so that he could tell her how much he loved her and prove to her that he could be the husband she had always wanted him to be.

Thapelo looked at his father where he sat crying. "Daddy," he called to him as he too began to cry.

Khutso looked at him, wiping away the tears.

"Daddy," Thapelo said, calling to him again.

Khutso opened his hand and Thapelo came to him and they embraced. "I love you, Thapelo," Khutso said, wiping away both his and Thapelo's tears. "At least I still have you."

"I love you too, Daddy."

\* \* \*

Filled with remorse, Khutso drove to Pretty's grave night after night in a sea of tears. He always knew what he wanted to say when he left the house, but when he got to the grave he never knew how to make sense of his thoughts. He would simply start to cry, holding on to the fresh soil as if Pretty was the soil and the soil, somehow, Pretty.

\* \* \*

Three weeks after her death, Khutso packed Pretty's belongings into a box. In her handbag he found her diary. Pretty had glued a picture of Thapelo and Khutso onto the cover with the caption *Everything for my family* written below it. Inside, on the New Year's Resolution page, she had written, *I have to celebrate all the birthdays of the people that I love and buy each of them a present.*

Khutso read it page by page. The last entry was on Wednesday, 13 March 2002: *I AM HIV POSITIVE.*

The test certificate, confirming that she was HIV positive, had been glued to the same page.

Khutso looked at it for hours, shaking his head, licking his suddenly dry lips. He cursed the day he had fallen for her tricks. How naïve I had been to ever think that she would make a wife, he thought.

Finally, he turned around and his eyes locked with Thapelo's. Khutso hadn't heard him calling him.

"Daddy?" Thapelo said.

They say that it's pointless to get angry with people who are dead, because they can't feel your anger. But Thapelo was alive, he was Pretty's son, and for a moment Khutso wanted to cut him into pieces very slowly to make him feel the pain that he was feeling.

"Daddy, can we go for a drive, please?" Thapelo asked.

Khutso looked at his son and paused, fighting to remain calm, to control his anger. "No," he finally said, looking away from Thapelo.

But Thapelo didn't pick up the warning signs. "Dad, let's go for a drive, please," he said.

"No!" Khutso shouted, his voice hard, and it was then that Thapelo knew that all was not well with his father. He wanted to ask him what was going on, but he had never seen his dad so angry. Khutso would sometimes beat him or shout at him, but two minutes later they would always be in each other's arms as if nothing had happened. This was different.

"Go away," Khutso said. "Go play your games. Leave me alone."

Thapelo turned and walked to his room as tears made their way out of his eyes.

Three days later his father was still a stranger, and a week after that Khutso took Thapelo out of his primary school. Though Thapelo's teachers tried to stop Khutso moving his son away, there was nothing they

p and Thapelo soon found himself dumped in an exclusive
school. After that, the only time his father remembered Thapelo was when the school officials called to complain about his be-
haviour or to ask for his tuition fees. He arranged for his sister to take
care of his son during the holidays, made sure that all his other needs
were taken care of by Pretty's younger sister Kgahliso, and with that he
cut Thapelo out of his life.

Currency
of charisma?

## 12

I. I live amongst you, waiting like a predator. I am faceless. I am mindless and thoughtless. But I am feared and despised. You hate me. But then I put on a face – wear a human face – and I am respected, appreciated and valued. I am I.

You lovingly summon me. I don't break in. My schemes are not like that. I am willingly invited in, and only then do I take up my position and do my work. Don't get me wrong, I love my work – it is my work and I do it with pride – but I do it in the most gentle of ways.

Many think that I am only for the poor, and that I will never come for them, but I am walking with two legs amongst you. Smiling back at your smile. Laughing at your jokes. You can think that I am not coming for you, but I will eat you out and leave what's left of you for death.

Do you think that because you are cautious I will not come for you? Do you think that those whose company I enjoy are only the foolish? Well, you are wrong. Your time is coming. I am coming especially for you. I am scheming my way into your system. That is my promise to you. I will find a way to get to you.

I am alive, but I have no dreams or visions; I have only a purpose. Sometimes I am very poor and sometimes I am very wealthy, but most of the time I am just I. That face, that man, that woman is me. You define me and give me all types of names. You try to understand me. But I like the game that you are all playing, talking about me as if you can identify me – thinking that I am a virus when I am out walking in the street. You have never seen my face. You think that the bony remains

charisma?

77

that are breathing their last look like me, but they are bones that I have long deserted. They are no longer of any use to me. I have long moved on.

I am coming for you. This is a promise. I promise you that I am coming for you.

# 13

Khutso was a wealthy man. Pretty's two life insurance policies had paid out, and although they had never had any financial difficulties, he now knew he never need worry about money again. But despite his new-found wealth, Khutso lived in the valley of suicide for weeks after Pretty's death.

When Pretty had been alive he had never thought that he would ever be able to understand someone who wanted to commit suicide. He had read about a man who had taken a gun and shot his two children while they were sleeping, before shooting his wife and then turning the gun on himself. At the time he couldn't understand what the man had been thinking. How could someone do something like that because of some temporary situation in his life? Khutso had wondered. What the fuck was he thinking? He had never found any logic in the man's actions, but he remembered him as he was walking in the valley and, finally, he understood his logic. Some things can make you take a gun and blow your own brains out, he realised.

Khutso roamed the valley and a thousand times came one step away from the exit. His senses ceased to pick up the sights and sounds of life. Hurt and failure became the only things that they communicated to him. His ears heard them. His tongue tasted them. His skin felt them. His eyes saw only them. The only way to have peace was to shut his body down, and the only way to do that was to die.

Then, one day, Khutso found himself sitting in his house, looking at the wall. Four days had passed since he had had anything to eat or drink, but he hadn't noticed; all he could think of was his pain. "What the fuck was I thinking?" he asked himself out loud, turning his head away from the wall and closing his eyes. Then he blamed his body. "What did you need her for?" He smacked his head with his right hand. "I am as good as dead."

He stood up. Then he sat down. He put both his hands on his head and cursed Pretty. Then he cursed her mother and father.

Finally, Khutso started to sob again, but he had no more tears. "Pretty, I will kill you!" he cried out, getting to his feet and putting up his fists as a tear slid slowly from his eye. "Pretty! Fuck you, bitch! I will kill you!" he yelled, beginning to throw punch after punch at the air in front of him. His eyes were closed, but he could see her in his mind.

It seemed to Khutso that Pretty was backing off. The coffee table blocked his way, but he kicked it aside as if it was nothing and cornered her against the wall. Then he started punching her. "Bitch, you are very lucky you died before I knew, I would have cut you to pieces . . . !" he shouted.

But it wasn't long before Khutso ran out of energy. He took a step back and opened his bloody hands, looking at them and then back at the wall he had been punching. His vision began to blur. He tried to lift his right leg, but instead he fell face first into the wall, sliding down to the floor slowly, blood dripping out of his nose and mouth – lights out.

* * *

Lights up – Khutso came back to life. Something had possessed him and made everything that had happened to him irrelevant. It's okay, it This is life. What has happened doesn't matter. What matis is life and it is for the living. It has to be lived.

And that was the way that Khutso left the valley of suicide – alive. It was as if it, the voice, had patted him on the shoulder, offered him a hand and helped him to his feet.

This is life, the voice continued, we are born, we live and then we die: life.

Khutso looked down at his chest. "It is life, we are born, we live and then we die: life," he repeated, feeling the need to say the words that filled his thoughts out loud.

Now have a bath and then let us live your life to your death.

For the first time in a month, Khutso smiled. Suddenly it felt good that he was still alive, and after four days without food or water he finally noticed that he was hungry and thirsty. He dragged himself to the refrigerator and fed his body, and when he had regained some of his energy he made his way to the bathroom to wash himself with his bruised and bloodied hands.

# 14

Khutso wanted a special kind of journal. He went from one stationery store to another, trying to explain what he wanted, but he couldn't find what he was looking for. "I want something leather-covered, like a Bible, with the same quality paper as a Bible," he told a saleslady one day, after she had shown him what they had.

"Why don't you go to a printer and ask them to do it the way you want it," she suggested to him.

Khutso thanked the saleslady and did as she had advised him. Then, finally, he had what he wanted: a leather-covered journal with five hundred unnumbered pages – each page divided into two columns – and two golden pages at the beginning and two at the end. The only words were embossed on the front cover in twenty-three carat gold: *Book of the Dead.*

"This is the most unusual request I have ever had," the sales manager told Khutso when he went to collect the book. "And to tell you the honest truth, it's the first job this company has ever done for a black man. Believe me, because I have worked here for thirty years."

The man went on to tell Khutso about all the special books that the company had made, and all the special people they had made them for, but Khutso knew that he was avoiding the question he really wanted to ask. "In case you are wondering what I am going to do with the book," Khutso finally said, making his way towards the door, "I am going to record my paternal family history; the male lineage from 1840 to the present day."

"Book of the Dead," the sales manager said, unable to pretend he was anything but relieved. "And here I was thinking that you are a serial killer, and you wanted to record the names of your victims."

"The black man is always a suspect . . ." Khutso replied, watching as shame stole over the sales manager's face.

* * *

Outside the printer's offices, Khutso sat in his car with the book on his lap. It was as if he was introducing himself to the book, and the book was introducing itself to him. He remembered that in his high school days all the troublemakers had been blacklisted in a book like the one that he now had before him. Ngwan'Zo's name had been written in the book in the first months of their third year of high school and Maoto's a few months after that. Khutso wondered how his life would have turned out if his name too had been written in that book.

# Book of the Dead

And every bitch I ever loved, I wish an Aids-related death.

*Goodenough Mashego*

I wrote it in the middle of the first golden page. I underlined it. He had taken the words right out of my mouth.

# Khutso

The honour of being the first entry in this great book went to Khutso. In the middle of the second golden page I wrote:

*03 October 2002: Khutso*
*Age: 41 years*
*Height: 1.74 metres*
*Weight: 107.6 kilograms*
*Status: HIV positive*
*CD4 count: 650*

We were sitting in Khutso's study, both of us pondering the mission ahead, the mission that we were going to undertake together. We are going to fuck 'em dead, I told him, and he smiled.

# Thabiso

Thabiso was the second to make it into my holy book. She just fell right in without any hassle.

"You are leaving town?" she asked Khutso, even though she already knew that he was leaving Polokwane – she had read my resignation letter. "What is it with you people and Gauteng?"

"South Africa is in Gauteng," Khutso replied, and that was where it began.

Thabiso was a married woman with a child, she had a degree and drove a top-of-the-range sports car, but she had no morals and no respect for her husband – theirs was a marriage made in the bank. She had been after Khutso since she'd laid eyes on him, but he had been married to Pretty and so he had run from her, but that afternoon the running came to an end. I took her. And afterwards I entered her details in the column on the left-hand side of the page:

> *05 October 2002: Thabiso*
> *Done.*
> *Early lunch, Oasis Lodge. Power is nothing without control.*

\*   \*   \*

Although Thabiso had a beautiful face, she was tall and fat with huge breasts. She always complained about her body, and she told Khutso that she had tried to diet many times, but she had failed each and every time. Wasn't it funny that I was the one to give her the body that she had always wanted, the body that she had wasted hours in the gym trying to get?

"You look wonderful," Khutso told her a few months later. "Don't you feel good, lively, full of life?"

But she quickly knew the truth, though she thought that she was infecting Khutso, not knowing that they were soldiers under the same command.

\* \* \*

Thabiso. I am in your blood and your heart pumps the death that I am to every corner. I have taken a bite of you and I will slowly take another one. You are my Cape apple, and I am going to eat you down to the core before I chuck you away.

My advice: blame it on your husband. Chances are that he was cheating on you anyway.

What are you thinking? I know, you are thinking about a miracle. You think that I will go away if you believe in the Almighty and go to church every Sunday, if you pray every second. But you are wrong. It is all useless. It is all futile.

\* \* \*

Later I heard that she was dead, so I filled in the right-hand column:

*Died: 16 December 2004*
*Cause of death: suicide*
*She could not handle the facts. Powerful woman. Disgrace of a wife.*

91

# Demie

A few months after moving Thapelo into the boarding school Khutso changed cities – moving from Polokwane to Tshwane. It was then that I decided that Khutso needed a makeover. He was dull, and for our purposes he needed to be a star – to stand out in a crowd. So, when we got to Tshwane the first thing we did was to lose the hair, the beard and moustache, lose his dull clothes and put on something vibrant, something that communicated with people. For our plan to work everyone had to want to associate with Khutso just by looking at him, he had to be a model on a catwalk.

In Gauteng we did away with the reliable Japanese car and bought something that was more than a car. Khutso loved the classic Voroso, so we got a '98 model, blue in colour, and put in a sound system – worth twice the value of the car.

Then, and only then, we were ready.

* * *

Khutso and I walked into an exclusive restaurant in Rosebank. In the corner five men were sharing a table and at first I thought that they were gay, but then Khutso noticed one of them. He was definitely a product of the University of the North – Khutso recognised him – and so we had to shake his hand.

They weren't gay, I was wrong, they were five educated black men: one from UDW, one from Wits and the other three from the University of the North. Kevin was the Wits graduate, Patrick was from UDW and

Mahlale, Ntsako and Cline were Khutso's fellow University of the North graduates. They were family men – Ntsako had four children, Cline had two and the others had one apiece – with homes in the suburbs. Four of their wives were also university graduates. Ntsako was the only one with a less educated woman, but of all of them she was the most ambitious – she worked as a nurse but was studying part-time through the University of South Africa. I considered this ambition a result of her jealousy of the other wives.

These husbands – and wives – were a clan. Family friends, they came together once a month, always in the third week of the month. Third week? I thought it was because by then their financial tanks were close to empty – typical black families, always living beyond their means.

Anyway, the reason that they were in an exclusive restaurant in Joburg was that they were on their way to the Durban Derby, filling up before driving to Durbs.

It worked like this: Ntsako and Cline were responsible for their accommodation in Durbs – they had booked two rooms. Mahlale was the logistics man – to and from Durban. And all the expenses in Durban would be covered by what was in Patrick and Kevin's pockets – that was their budget.

"Why not fly?" I asked. "You'll get there in an hour."

"Everything has a financial implication, my friend," Patrick replied.

Then I volunteered to fly them there and back and hire them a car in Durbs, just to show them that although we might have graduated from the same university, they were still boys. And with that I bought exclusive rights to the role of dominant male in their clan.

Let's be clear, it was not soccer fever that was calling them to Durban. No. If you are into nightlife, then Durban nights are for you. Married life can't give you soccer fever like Durban nights. Making love to your wife and fucking a woman are two different things, and for these married men this was what the Durban trips were all about – enjoying their sexual passions. For these guys there was nothing better than that wild animal thing of being a lone bull in a herd of buffalo during mating season.

They were an unofficial team and they had complete trust in their coach "god-condom".

"You are our friend," Mahlale told Khutso. "You are valuable to us and to your family and relatives. You are a vital part of the nation. You are a father. In short, you are a man. But as a man you also have a man's needs. So, your strongest point is that you are a man and your weakest point is the fact that you are a man. And, as a man, it would be tragic beyond words if you were to take a disease from the street and deliver it into your home."

The others nodded their heads in unison.

"I have lost too many friends and relatives to HIV," Mahlale continued, "and I don't want to lose any more, but my problem is that I am a man and I can't stop being what I am . . ."

"We can't stop being what we are," Ntsako added. "We can't stop being men. Our forefathers enjoyed their women freely, but we can't. We are in danger. But, unlike our forefathers, we have our god: god-condom."

Then each of them gave me a pack of condoms and it felt like I was being initiated into the team.

"They will save your life," Ntsako added. "They have saved this life of mine many times."

* * *

We were in Durban for the Top Eight cup final. Khutso had played soccer at school and loved it, but I was bored to death. I sat there pretending to watch the game until I couldn't take it any more. Then I decided to wash the boredom away, and by the time we got out of the stadium I had the number of one of the soccer-crazy girls that were sitting in front of us.

Demie. She became my first Durban conquest, and in the process of bedding her Khutso impressed the boys with his smooth moves. Six men walked into the stadium and came out with three women, but my flower of choice played harder to get than the others. Mahlale and Ntsako bedded her friends, but she wasn't ready. "We just met, don't take me like that," she said, demanding respect.

We kissed and she even let me touch the fertile grounds, but that was all. "That is not me. I don't do that," she said.

So on my first Durban morning after my first Durban night, I kept my vigil over her. Khutso wanted to let her go, but that wasn't necessary. This, I told him, is the last kick of a dying horse – then we will be in control.

Demie. She was twenty-seven, the mother of a six-year-old boy and, by profession, the PA to some manager in some part of Durban municipality. She had her own town house and a nanny to look after her son. I found it funny that she didn't want to let me in, because I always thought that single moms got into bed with whomever they felt the need to get into bed with, but she played hard to get.

Two weeks later, after hours on the phone, I flew to Durban just for her. She was finally ready.

In Durban I was introduced to her son, Sandile, a six-year-old fashionista. Everything Sandile wore was expensive, and Khutso immediately remembered a time, years earlier, when he had thought it a waste of money to buy his child expensive things. He looked at the boy. What a waste, he thought.

I played the father figure and swept the boy off his feet. We went for a drive – just the two of us – and I taught him how to drive a car, a way to get through to any boy. Then we went to the shopping mall and I bought him another expensive pair of sneakers. Finally, we went to an amusement arcade and played games until his mother called me, worried that we had been gone too long.

"Mummy, look at my new shoes," Sandile said as soon as we got back to his mother's town house, and I wondered how many of her boyfriends had played the father figure with him just to get her to open the doors to her fortress.

"Wow!" she said, and at that moment I knew I had captured her heart.

"Uncle Khutso bought them for me, do you like them?"

"He put the sneakers on in the shop and wouldn't take them off," I said. "I hope you don't mind that I bought them for him."

But Sandile didn't give his mother a chance to respond – he was busy trying to give her a full report of everything we had done in two minutes flat. When he had finally calmed down it was time to work on his mother and get what we came for, and it wasn't long before we got it.

"I don't like what you are doing to Sandile," she said when we were lying on her queen bed, catching our breath after the long haul.

I knew she loved it, so I did not respond.

"I mean, I love it," she continued, "but it has a psychological effect, especially if you are not staying long."

"Who said I'm not staying?" I asked. "I am staying. I want to stay."

Which was the truth. I was already inside and making myself comfortable. I was going nowhere.

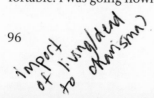

Obviously, Khutso wasn't staying. No, he wasn't staying at all. He was on a quest. He had a much bigger cause. But I was there to stay until death would us part.

# Jarush

I was a scavenger, gorging myself on anything, everything. Every time the clan went to Durban – from Friday night, when we landed, to Sunday morning – I gorged myself on anything with breasts. I loved it.

After a while I began to leave the team in Joburg, they were a poor bunch after all, and would fly to Durban to enjoy the Durban nights alone. And that was when I found my Indian queen. Her parents called her Jarush, but I called her Jar. She was the receptionist at the Garden Court – my Durban home from home. She didn't want anything but condoms on, but then she came to Tshwane and entered my fortress.

The house we – Khutso and I – bought in Tshwane had been designed in a way that would capture any woman's heart, and it wasn't long before it captured hers. Like all women, she looked around carefully for evidence of another female, but she didn't find it. Women like to mark their territory. Every one of them who spent time in the house left something behind – underwear, shoes, make-up – with the intention of warning any other woman who came to the house that the space was already taken, but we always returned whatever they left behind or threw it away.

"You live here alone?" Jar finally asked.

"Yes, and that is the sad part, but it ends today," I lied. "I want to live here with you. Please. I want to share my life with you." I got down on my knees. "Jar, marry me. Let me father your children."

"I don't know what to say," she said, wiping away the tears that had suddenly sprung into her eyes.

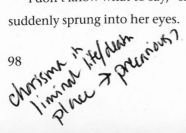

"I am committed to you," I said. "I want you." Then I got up off my knees and kissed her, and she forgot about safe sex and joined my legion.

\* \* \*

Jar came and stayed for two weeks and every day, as always, I came home after eleven, claiming that I was working late. That was until she thought that she would surprise me with a special supper for two at the office. I was nowhere to be found, so she called me. "Where are you?" she asked.

"Jar, I am at the office. I'm sorry. I know, I know, but I have deadlines to meet."

She did not respond and I knew that there was something wrong. "I am coming," I said. "I am very sorry. I forgot to call."

It was almost as if I could see the tears that were running down her cheeks. "Stop lying," she finally said.

"What?" I asked. I knew that she was hurting. "What's wrong? I will be there in a moment."

"Khutso, I am at your office."

By then I had been thinking for a while that it was about time that she left. I was done with her. She should go back to Durban. "Jar, please go home, I am coming back home right now," I said and cut the call.

By the time I got home from recruiting for my legions in Sunnyside, it was half past one and she was more than fed up – she didn't want to hear anything I had to say. "Don't talk. Don't say anything," she said, trying to control her anger. "I don't want you to say anything. Don't you understand that?"

Then she went online and booked a ticket back to Durban – an early flight. She left Khutso. But I left with her.

# Matimba

It's funny, the average black student doesn't have a car, but when there's a bash on any campus the parking area is always full to capacity. Here in the province of gold we, the team, joined those who prowl the campuses, and wherever there was a swarm of young women we were sure to show up in convoy.

Khutso knew that it was possible, but before he met the team he had never had a one-hour stand. By then we had had our fair share of one-night stands, but a one-night stand doesn't come close to a one-hour stand. A one-hour stand is when you pick up a girl on the dance floor, fuck her and then walk away like nothing happened – no number, no nothing.

At Soshanguve – the former TNT, now TUT – Khutso had two one-hour stands. The first girl he never even spoke to. I saw her across the room, moving to the beats. She knew I was looking at her and she was enjoying it. I smiled. She smiled. She was leading me on and I responded. Then she came close. She thought that Khutso couldn't dance. She thought that he was going to be a pole – a dancing pole. Then Khutso showed the children that they had not invented the dance floor. That sealed the deal and he took her by the hand and she followed him to her slow execution in the toilet.

The second execution took place in Khutso's car. But this execution turned out to be a reinfection in both directions. It was a war between two great soldiers of the cause and, needless to say, it was full of mind-blowing thrills.

\* \* \*

100

Over time Khutso's house became a sort of brothel. The team would come back to our place with their girls and bed them there. Often they would bring back six girls and we would rotate. But this team believed in the god-condom. "This is for enjoyment, not for reproduction," Ntsako would always say, handing out condoms left and right before the battle commenced.

I would bed all six without protection, but the team tormented me, playing hard to get with their god-condom. It seemed like there was no way of getting to them, and, oh, how I wanted to get to them! It ate away at me. I needed a way to get to them.

Then Khutso said something. "They have wives," he said.

\* \* \*

She seemed to be the kind of woman who grew up in a conservative family – respectful; the kind to put her husband and children first.

"You are wearing . . . ?" I asked Mahlale's wife at one of their clan gatherings.

She smiled.

"I know it cost an arm, a leg and a limp, but it's as if he designed it especially for you. You look . . ." I lacked the appropriate word.

"Stunning?" she asked.

"No, that is not the word. Stunning doesn't do it. You deserve to be on the cover of *Vogue*."

"You should tell that to Mahlale," she said. "He thinks that it's a waste of money."

Money: the key to any woman's heart.

"You remind me, I have a voucher at home," I continued. "There is nothing for me in their new collection. Maybe you could pick up something . . ."

"Really? I would really appreciate it."

"I'll let Mahlale know that I'm giving it to you," I said cautiously. "You know males and their egos. Maybe I should give it to him and he can buy you . . ."

"Let me worry about him," she said, cutting me short. "I deal with his ego every day."

I let time pass. A month passed and in that time I didn't say anything about the voucher. I waited to see how much she really wanted it. We met twice that month, but she didn't say anything about the promise I had made on either occasion. The third time we met was at another gathering of the clan. I had been invited too, as a friend.

That afternoon the men stood outside drinking and talking about politics, economic development and every now and then – in code – about their concubines. Meanwhile, inside, the women were preparing braai pap for the occasion. I passed them in the kitchen on my way to the loo, and when I came back they took the opportunity that presented itself.

"When are you getting married?" one of them asked.

"And who is the lucky woman?" another chipped in.

"Before she died I promised my wife that I would never get married again," I said.

They paused. "That is very brave," one of them said.

"That is so sweet," another added as the thought washed over her and brought tears to her eyes.

"Sweet?" Matimba, Ntsako's wife (the nurse), said disapprovingly. "He is a man. If Ntsako died I wouldn't get married again, but he is a man . . ." She paused. "You are a man," she said, turning to me. "You need a woman."

"Well, actually I did find somebody," I said.

"You did?" they chorused, neither surprised nor as happy as they pretended to be.

"Yes, but she was happily married," I went on. "And so my search continues, and the prospect of finding the right woman grows dimmer with each passing year . . ."

"Spokie, Spokie," Ntsako said, addressing me as he walked into the kitchen, "the men are outside, and we need to hear your political views."

A few days earlier – we had been in Durbs, enjoying another of its mind-blowing nights – Ntsako had made it clear that he didn't trust me any more. He had said it loud and clear. "I don't trust you, not because you did anything, just because I don't trust men of your calibre. You don't smoke, you don't drink and you have no steady girlfriend. Then, to top it all, you are softly spoken. Sorry, Khutso, but I don't trust you. You are a phantom."

After that he had taken to calling me Spokie and now, by using the nickname in front of them, he was showing the wives that he didn't trust me.

"You want to hear my political views," I said. "Well then, let me go and air my political views for the good of this beautiful country of ours."

But it was at that moment, as we walked out of the kitchen – Ntsako behind me as if he was herding me into a barn – that Mahlale's wife called out to me to remind me of the promise that I had made.

"Oh, that . . ." I said. "I'm sorry, I forgot about it. I'll drop it off sometime."

Then, during the week, she called me, just to remind me again about the voucher. I told her that I would deliver it to her at work, but in the end – after visiting Sandton City and making up a fifteen-thousand-rand voucher – I left it at reception.

Why fifteen grand? Because that was her salary level.

103

Mahlale's wife called me later that day. She wasn't pleased that I had left the voucher at reception. She had wanted to see me. "Sorry, I was in a hurry," I said and cut the call.

What happened next is pure speculation, but this is my best guess. First, Mahlale's wife called the shop and they told her the value of the voucher. Then, during the week, she called the other wives and they all made plans to go shopping that weekend – a little retail therapy. Finally, the thing that I had feared happened. Ntsako found out about the voucher and he didn't like it, he didn't like it at all. He immediately called a meeting of the team – minus Mahlale – and they agreed unanimously that they needed to tell me to stop what I was doing.

"I don't feel that I did anything wrong," I said to Ntsako when he called me on my cellphone. "And if I offended you, I am very sorry."

Then I called Mahlale. "Mahlale, I made a mistake," I said. "A big mistake. I saw your wife wearing something from the place I usually buy my clothes, and I ended up giving her a voucher that I had. At the time I did not know that . . ."

"She told me about it," he said, cutting me short.

"I am sorry."

"It is nothing."

*  *  *

Fly-fishing. Once the able fisherman has cast his line – after feeding his ears with the sound of the flying hook and line, and watching both hook and line break the surface of the still water – he can do nothing but wait. So I waited.

Matimba, Ntsako's wife, called me about a month after the debacle. "You don't come around any more," she said. "What did we do to you?"

"You really want to know why?" I asked.

"I'm curious."

"It's because you all think that I slept with Mahlale's wife . . ." I paused to let the words sink in. "And anyway, what if I did? What happens under the cover of night is of the night." I paused. The trout was not out of the water yet, but it had taken the bait and I was carefully reeling it in.

"I am sorry," she said.

"And I forgive you. Anyway, how are you doing?"

After that Matimba called us every day, late in the morning, and we talked.

"It is just unfortunate my daughter is only twelve," she said one morning. "If she was nineteen or twenty I would give her to you." She said it like she meant it.

"Really?" I asked.

"I mean it."

The trout was in the net. "And what if she didn't love me?"

"Women don't love men. All we want out of a man is security and comfort, security above all. That is what we need, then we learn to love, to accept the man as a husband and father. If you gave her security and comfort, she would love you."

Matimba only ever called us in the late morning till one Friday when the lure of the Durban nights became too much for Ntsako. The excuse – SuperSport against Sundowns. I didn't know they were in Durbs, but when she called late in the evening it was clear that her man wasn't home.

"Can I come see you?" I asked.

"No," she said. "My children are home."

I didn't respond, making the silence seem like the saddest thing she had ever heard.

"I am sorry," she apologised.

I felt like God.

"Tomorrow?" she asked.

"Matimba, I will die waiting . . ."

We continued with the conversation, and a little later I asked her to close her eyes and touch herself here and there. She agreed reluctantly, obviously feeling uneasy, but she was into it soon enough and later she confessed that she had never felt as good.

* * *

Saturday. Matimba drove herself from Noordwyk to Pretoria and we met in the underground parking area at the State Theatre, where she parked her car. She was looking wonderful and the only turn-off was that she was wearing too much make-up. Khutso hates too much make-up, but in terms of our mission this was no obstacle.

In bed Matimba was like a tiger taking down an elephant, which was something I had come to expect from wayward wives.

"Why are you wearing full panties?" I asked her afterwards. "It's so old school, and you would look fabulous in a G-string."

"He doesn't like them . . ." she responded.

"What? You are joking."

"He says that they are degrading to women."

"He loves them," I said, trading away his secrets. "They make his blood boil every time . . ."

* * *

When I feel good about something, it always seems to me like it is the first time I have ever felt good in this life of mine. Bedding Matimba was an achievement and it saturated me with good feelings. As I wrote her

106

name in the book of books, I wondered how she would play the card I had dealt her. I hoped that she would play it the right way:

25 October 2003: Matimba
Believe it, curiosity kills.

And then I smiled, knowing that it was only a matter of time before things would begin to fall apart.

* * *

Matimba didn't play the card in the way that I had expected her to play it. The other wives didn't know of her stolen Saturdays, when their husbands were lured by the Durban nights. I had thought that she would whisper in their ears and then curiosity would kill them all, but I was wrong, her jealousy of the other wives made her keep her secret to herself.

Three months later Matimba finally graduated and I was invited to the big celebration at their suburban home. I was not surprised to find Ntsako even more suspicious of me than before. "Spokie, I don't trust you," he said, drunk and less than happy to see me. "I have never trusted you."

It didn't matter any more, I thought as we celebrated his wife's graduation. He was dying, he just didn't know it yet.

After the graduation party the calls from Matimba just stopped. Chickens were roasting, I thought. I am not sure who discovered the good news first, but they were both guilty and it didn't matter who blamed who, what was done was done. Ntsako so trusted in the god-condom that I am sure he must have been convinced that he didn't come home with it. He had never slipped up, not even once. He had always been extra careful, and he must have looked at Matimba with burning eyes, retracing his conquests, knowing that she must have cheated on him.

Maybe she broke down. Maybe she gave herself away somehow. Whatever the chain of events, when the police finally came to rescue her she was already lifeless. Later, one of the cops told me that Ntsako had cursed Khutso's name all the way to the holding cells, vowing that he was going to kill him with his bare hands, as in the heat of his violence Matimba had called out Khutso's name.

And, sure enough, when he got out of jail – after spending only twelve hours inside – Ntsako went back home and picked up his gun. Then he drove to Tshwane. But when he got to where Khutso lived, he had to tell security who he was there to see. So he lied. They called Khutso. "Mahlale is here at the gate," the guard told him.

Mahlale always called before coming over to our house, so Khutso knew immediately that something was wrong. "Tell him I'm not home," he told the security guard.

But Ntsako forced his way in. He pulled out his gun and drove his car through the boom as the security guards took cover.

As he parked his car in our driveway I looked at him and smiled. He was foaming at the mouth, the gun shaking in his right hand. Shame, see what I can do to a sane man, I told Khutso. It's the effect that I have on some people. Fuck you, Ntsako, where is your god-condom now? I wanted to ask him. Why don't you put him on? He has saved you countless times. Maybe he can perform one last miracle.

Ntsako went around the house, but all the doors were locked. Eventually, he broke a window and climbed in, but Khutso jumped from the balcony and seconds later the police arrived. Khutso told them that there was nobody else in the house and so they just waited for Ntsako to come out. I was hoping that he would shoot himself dead, but he finally came out of the house, looking tired and worn, and the police handcuffed him and put him in a car. I looked at him as he sat there, waiting to be taken away. As I watched, he laughed a little laugh and shook his head, and at that moment I remembered a Tswana saying: leso segolo ke disego (the greatest death is laughing). And right then and there I believed it. He was laughing at himself because there was nothing he could do but laugh.

Later I awarded Ntsako an honorary entry in the book of books:

*25 May 2004: Ntsako*
*You said it: "Your strongest point is that you are a man and your weakest point is the fact that you are a man."*

\* \* \*

Later that day I drove to Mopani Street in Noordwyk. It is a quiet street full of trees; a street that has serenity. I parked the car and we sat there for a while. Matimba was dead, but the other wives had lived to tell the tale. And that is fortunate for them, I told Khutso, but I am still walking around. The hook is still in the water. Their time is coming.

# I

I have been talked about so much that people say my name like it belongs in a nursery rhyme. They have seen so many pictures of dying people that they eat their evening meal in front of the TV, undisturbed by the reports on the news. They have seen me take down gladiators – eat them up, put them in bed and leave them wearing nappies – and yet they are still not afraid. I have become . . . usual.

These people, they are so intelligent that they think I will never come for them. Or maybe they think that when I come for them I will knock first, identify myself and then wait for a response . . .

I take a very straight and determined mind, work it over, and create complete confusion in it. I take a beautiful creature, work it over, and turn it into something of no aesthetic value. When they recognise my work, some start to look to God, and others put all their hopes in a traditional doctor, but it doesn't really matter which you choose, they are both full of lies.

Soon, when people look at you, you will start to think that they can see me in your face. When you catch people talking about you, and they pause their conversation, you will think that they are really talking about me. You will start to stigmatise yourself. In reality, by the time they start to see the telltale signs of me in your face I will be long gone, because by then you are no longer of any use to me. You are deteriorating, full-blown, and you can't hide the truth any more.

"I have been diagnosed with some mysterious disease," you will say.

But they can see through your lie.

110

"Oh! That old witch has sent her thing," you will say.

But they can see through your lie.

There are those brave enough to say it out loud. "I am HIV positive," they say.

Their friends will admire their bravery, but they will still be concerned about their safety when they shake hands, and the women who used to hug them will suddenly prefer a handshake.

Then I have no use for you any longer. You are no longer fit to do what I desire of you. I need you when you are at your best; when you have passion for life, when you have dreams and are chasing them hard. That is when I need you, because you can do a great deal of good work for me. I don't need you when you are trying to avoid your friends in case they see what you imagine is me in your face.

Is there a break/space/crack btwn SD + charisma? What is here?

function of silence?
↓
Silence + Violence?
↓
Silence + power or weakness?

# Jessica, Michelle and Candy

I was driving down the road in a top-of-the-range vehicle. A few months earlier a motor journalist had written that "it turns the road into a catwalk", and, sure enough, wherever I drove everyone noticed me. The motor journalist had also said that it was a weekend car (probably because he couldn't afford one), but I was using it each and every day to prowl the streets, looking to recruit soldiers to expand my empire.

My left hand lay on the armrest as I drove, my right hand holding the wheel lightly as the number one kwaito song – played very softly – washed over me. Uzoyithola kanjani uhleli ekhoneni (How can you get it, sitting on the corner?)

The prey were in the streets, ready to be preyed upon, and in the distance I spotted three young girls. They were my friends: bored and looking to substitute boredom for a good time. They had spotted me as well and stopped their conversation in the hope that I wouldn't pass them by. We locked eyes as I passed them. "Can I pick you up?" my eyes asked.

"Pick us up," their eyes responded.

I stopped a few metres down the road and waited, looking at them in the mirrors.

They seemed to want to run to the car, but one was more cautious than the others; something held her back. Her conscience? She should have listened.

I didn't call them – that's inexperience – and eventually they came of their own free will, following each other like goats.

I opened the doors for them and looked each one of them in the eye reaper's garden?

as they got into the car, two in the back and one in front. "Hones speaking, no lies," I said. "Because I am a man who tells it like it is, and I hope that you are women who like to hear it as it is."

I looked deep into the eyes of the one in the front seat. Her stomach was bare and her braless breasts were on display. "I am bored and looking for a good time," I continued, reaching out and running my hand against her flat stomach. "Are you all looking for a good time?"

They didn't say anything, but the one in the front seat allowed me to reach down into her shorts to the fertile soil where one can only plant a life.

"Can I take you all somewhere where we can all have a good time and be naughty with each other, get drunk and naked?" I asked.

They responded as if I was tickling them – they giggled and smiled.

"You have the driving power and we are already in your car," the one in the front seat finally responded.

"Let's chase this boredom away and have a good time," I said.

\*   \*   \*

We cruised to a private game farm, enjoyed the views and the wildlife, and then we got a room. Khutso ordered the most expensive champagne there is, but my special guests didn't like it, so Khutso ordered them their choice of alcoholic beverages instead. Then we sat back and waited for the referee to blow the whistle so that the game could commence.

\*   \*   \*

They gave me fake names at the start, but twice Candy called Jessica by her real name and it startled them – amateurs. I didn't care, as I had no intention of seeing them again.

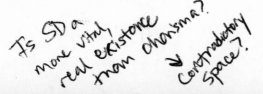
Is SD a more vital, real existence than charisma? Contradictory space?

Three against one. Some things Khutso had heard about and thought impossible, but I proved him wrong that afternoon.

Afterwards, I entered them into my book:

*12 June 2004: Jessica, Michelle and Candy*
*Extracting boredom from our lives. Done.*

# Reneilwe

Children these days try and behave like adults. They are not playful like Khutso was when he was their age. They know much more about the world than he knew.

She was pure and untainted. I am not sure what takes over men's minds when they look at a young girl in her final stage of metamorphosing into a woman, but I wish that I could freeze them all at that stage forever, and surely all women wish it too.

She was the little girl who lived with her mother in the house across the road from Khutso's. Twice I waved at her as I drove past. The third time I stopped the car. "Hello," I said when she came closer.

"Hi."

"Are you all right, my dear?" I asked her.

We were still talking when her mother arrived home and I was introduced for the first time to my next-door neighbour. "I always thought that the house was empty," she said when she found out that I lived across the street.

"Empty apart from me," I replied.

"Every time I saw you, you were busy in the garden. I thought that you were the garden boy and that the house was a holiday home for some wealthy people."

"Sorry, you were wrong," I said and laughed. "This is this garden boy's house."

"It is a beautiful house," she said.

I took them on a guided tour of the house.

"Wow! You live here all alone?" my next-door neighbour said, obviously taken with the house.

"I like your cars," her daughter said.

"I love my cars," I replied.

"I like the red one."

"You should drive it first and tell me if you still like it afterwards."

"I can't drive."

"Unfortunately."

"But you could take me for a ride."

With the permission of her mother we went for the drive. I pushed the car over the legal speed limit to show her what it could do – and it was an able car. Then we drove somewhere quieter and I put her in the driving seat. She cruised to thirty per hour, shaking and sweating in disbelief. Finally, she stopped in the middle of the road and gave me a hug and a kiss. "Do you know that it is illegal to kiss underage girls?" I asked her.

"I know, but it's not illegal for young girls to kiss an adult."

In Khutso Reneilwe found the father figure she had never had, the one that she had always wanted. Later she told him that a few photos and a VHS video that had been shot when she was a toddler were all she had ever known of her father for the first eleven years of her life.

"It is not that I don't want you to see him," her mother had told her when she asked about her father, "but don't you think that he knows only too well that he has a twelve-year-old daughter? And don't you think that I too need a husband? I need him as much as you, but I don't think that he needs us in any way. Why then should we run after him? I am tired of running after people."

But Reneilwe needed to see her father, if only just to make up her own mind about him, and so her mother tracked him down and set up a meeting with him. But it was just as her mother had said, and she came back hurt and confused. "Rolling stones just keep on rolling," her mother had said, trying to comfort her daughter. "So all we can do is to continue to live our lives and hope to live happily."

From that day on they never talked about her father again. But the meeting hadn't annulled Reneilwe's need for a father figure. The mother may have been able to move on, but the daughter still needed someone to fill that hole in her life, and despite the meeting she continued to hope that one day her father would roll back into their lives. She thought that her mother was bound to be a much happier person if she had a man around the place. This wasn't to say that they weren't happy – they were the happiest mother and daughter that there could be – but sometimes her mother would look at a family while they were out shopping together and make some comment which would wake up the ghosts.

Then I came along, and she found a father in me. She said that I was a lonely man and quickly took to calling me "the Lonely Man". I knew immediately that she wished that her mother and the Lonely Man would go out together. "Ma, you are a lonely mother of one, and he is a lonely man, staying alone and always in a hurry," I imagined her saying to her mother. "Why don't we . . ."

The day after the drive, Reneilwe invited the Lonely Man to come and have dinner with her and her lonely mother. Even though her mother was obviously doubtful about the whole scheme, Reneilwe somehow sweet-talked her into cooking dinner for me. "You are always alone," she said. "And we are always alone, me and my mum, so just come over to our house tonight. My mother, she always cooks wonderful food every day. Please come. You are our neighbour. We are neighbours."

Women + cooking?

117

Late that night I found myself at a table with two beautiful women, mother and daughter, each one a version of the other at another age. We were like a picture of the perfect family, the way life is supposed to be.

Reneilwe looked at her mother, then she looked at me and beamed as if she was the most blessed girl in the world.

"So what do you do?" Nomsa, Reneilwe's mother, asked.

"Ek is 'n prokureur."

"What is that?" the daughter asked.

"Prokureur is 'lawyer' in Afrikaans."

"Are all lawyers always as busy as you are?"

"I don't know, but I'm addicted to my work," I said. "My life is work. I need it to keep sane, so I work eighteen hours a day, sleep for four and try and relax for two, which is always hard to do unless I am at a table like this."

Their conversation was general and I saw no reason to ask them questions. "For a lawyer you don't ask many questions," Nomsa observed.

"That is because I spend my professional life asking questions, trying to get to the truth," I replied. "So I don't like to ask questions in real life. I believe that life should not be about questions and answers."

"Then what should it be about?" the mother asked.

"Life should be about listening and laughing. And I don't think that you can laugh at a question."

"Well, I am going to ask you one more question," she said. "You have the right not to reply, but I would like to know the answer." She paused. "Where is your woman?"

"You see, I can't laugh at that because questions are never funny."

"Sorry."

"We divorced," I said. "And I am not going to lie. I was definitely the

118

one to blame. She left because I was a terrible husband. She did all she could to hold us together, but I was never a husband, only ever a lawyer. Fortunately, we didn't have any children."

"Why not get married again?"

"I loved my ex-wife. I loved her and I haven't found a woman that I love as I loved her. And even if I did find a woman I loved enough to marry, I know that she would leave me too, because I don't know how to be a good husband. Why can't I be a better husband? Well, it is because I am addicted to my work. And that question you have on your face. Yes, I will survive without it. I have already survived for seven years without it, so why not seven more, why not a lifetime."

Nomsa smiled. "What question is that?" she asked.

"We are in the presence of a child," I replied. "Let's respect that."

Then I thought I should tell them a tale and make them laugh before I kissed them both good night. "Do you know that when I was young we didn't have a radio, let alone a TV?"

Reneilwe couldn't imagine a life like that.

"To entertain us my father and mother told us stories every night. When we were all gathered around the fire, they would say, 'Nonwane-nonwane'."

"Keleketla," Nomsa responded.

* * *

Reneilwe's mother trod softly – Nomsa knew this bumpy road, she had travelled it before and it was a road that she didn't really want to travel again – but her daughter trampled over everything eagerly. Reneilwe became my sunshine. She was beautiful, naïve, opinionated and saturated with life.

One afternoon a few days later, during yet another driving lesson,

Reneilwe stopped the car on the side of the road. "What is it that you have survived without for seven years?" she asked, looking at me keenly.

"I refuse to answer that question on the grounds that I wasn't talking to you," I replied and looked the other way, a smile playing on my face.

"It is sex, isn't it?" she said, her eyes shining knowingly. "Did you really survive that long without sex?"

Here was the chance that I had been waiting for. It was time to strike. "I refuse to answer that question on the grounds that I was not talking to you," I repeated.

"I know it is," she said. "You can deny it, but I know it is, I am not that foolish."

I kissed her. I touched her. Her pubic hair had only just sprouted and no thought of trimming it had ever entered her head.

"I was scared," she said afterwards.

"I am scared," I replied.

"I am a big girl."

"You are an underage girl."

The fact made her very angry, but she knew why I said it. She looked the other way, then she smiled the anger away. "If you are worried that I am going to tell," she said, "then don't worry, I won't tell. I am a big girl."

I knew she wouldn't tell, but I also thought that her mother would spot the telltale signs, so I bought three tickets to the Market Theatre and we washed away the evidence with a musical and a pizza.

I thought that I was going to let Reneilwe down slowly, but I lost control and she conquered me. What is it about a young female body in the final stages of moulding itself into a woman? Whatever it is, I couldn't get enough of it.

120

"My mother has a vibrator," she said one day when we were out on one of our drives.

I did not comment.

"I think that she is a lonely woman," she continued. "Life has been unfair to her."

"Didn't you say that she has a vibrator?" I said. "If she has a vibrator, then she must be satisfied in one department at least."

"It doesn't talk to her," she replied. "I think that they should make vibrators that can talk to lonely women as they satisfy them, don't you think?"

"Where is your father?"

"And I thought that you only asked questions in your professional capacity," she crowed. "That was an outright lie and my mother bought it. I can't believe she bought it! I can't believe it! I never thought she was that dumb." She mimicked me. "And that question you have on your face. Yes, I will survive without it. I have already survived for seven years without it, so why not seven more, why not a lifetime." She even made the hand gestures I had made. "I always thought my mother was more intelligent than that, but then again you are a prokureur, you lie under oath, don't you." She pointed at me and I smiled. "You still want to know about my father?" she asked.

"Yeah!"

"He is at home."

"At home?" I was puzzled.

"He is the vibrator, dummy."

"Did you ever . . ." I paused, searching for the right words, "use your father?"

"You are sick!" she said, drawing out the words. "How can you ask that about my father? Shit, that is the sickest thing I have ever been asked in all my life! How can you even think like that . . ." She was giggling. "No, no, no, I never used my father and I never will, but I can honestly say that however good he is, he can't be better than you, Lonely Man."

Reneilwe had presence, learned quickly and wanted to learn more. You could feel her learning. I wanted to be with her all the time. She was funny. She was full of life.

*  *  *

"Ma," Reneilwe asked one night, after an evening out, as we were walking to our cars, "is it possible that one day I will be able to call the Lonely Man father?" She was walking between us. "Don't you think we would make a great family? Maybe we were meant to be."

Her mother didn't respond and I didn't know what to say.

"Well, I don't care what you think," she continued. "I think that I have a mother and I think I have found a father, it's just that my mother and father haven't found each other yet."

"Maybe I am a father," I finally said, "but a husband? I don't think so."

She gave me a hug and kissed me good night. "Good night, Dad."

"Good night, baby." I hugged her mother. "Good night."

"Good night."

*  *  *

"Was I good yesterday or what?" she asked me the following afternoon.

"What?"

"The cover-up: 'Good night, Dad'. I am bad. I am bad, very bad."

"You are bad."

"I am a bitch."

*  *  *

Finally, the holidays ended and the child had to go back to school. "If you want to disgrace yourself, you can come and see me," she said on our last day together.

Somehow she left with a part of me, but the foundation that she had laid for me with her mother was strong, and Khutso and I promised each other that we would build on it while she was away.

# Nomsa

Nomsa and I got to know each other much better after Reneilwe went back to boarding school, and Nomsa got to know that lies are sweet. How sweet it is to lie to somebody who already knows the full extent of the lies that can pour out of the male heart and see her smile at those lies. I got to know her much better and she opened all the doors, even showing me the gap where her missing molar had once stood strong – old age creeping in.

We tried to ignore the attraction that had developed between us. I ignored it intentionally because ignoring it makes women value themselves and the relationship – the whole "he loves me because he is not trying to rush into sex" thing.

Then, when finally the inevitable happened, and we were into each other – at the point where words were just an irritation; her mouth half open and her eyes almost falling out – I stopped. "I think we are moving too fast," I said, standing up and shaking my head, enjoying the disappointment on her face.

"Y-yes," she stuttered, "yes, we are."

"Good night," I said, grabbing my jacket. "I am just going to run back to the office for a few things."

"You are going back to the office?" she asked, the irritation in her voice plain. It sounded as if she was saying, "You are leaving *me* to go back to the office?"

"Yes. I have to work."

"You should stop working and have some sweet sleep," she said.

"Sleep is for the poor," I replied, and she managed to smile. "Good night."

"Good night."

On the way to the office I thought that she had probably turned immediately to her unsatisfactory vibrator, and in response to that thought I called a client of mine, a young female. Khutso had handled her divorce, and ensured that she got a huge settlement. "I am leaving the office now and have nowhere to go," I told her. "Can I invite myself into your bed?"

"Do I have the right to say no?" she asked.

"No."

"Then why do you ask?"

And a few hours later she was counted as part of my legion.

* * *

I had showed Nomsa that I valued her and, finally, she had had enough of it. I could hear it in her tone when she called. "Please, come over tonight," she said. "I have cooked for you."

"I am working," I replied.

"Please," she begged.

When I got there she was wearing a silk nightdress. She closed the distance between us in a moment, came and stood so close to me that I could feel her breathing heavily on me. "Nomsa, what are you doing to me?" I asked. "Whatever it is, I can't handle it," I lied.

"We are both adults," she said, as if what was about to happen needed to be justified somehow and the fact that we were adults was that justification.

"It doesn't mean we are responsible," I responded.

"Let's be irresponsible," she whispered breathily.

I closed my eyes and we started kissing, but, suddenly, as if by magic, there in her hand was a packet of condoms. I have never cursed the motherfucker who invented the condom like I did in that moment, but I put one on and we ran the race.

Afterwards, I wanted to get out of her house as fast as I could – my mission had failed – but she wanted me to stay. She wanted us to hold each other. She wanted us to talk. She wanted everything a vibrator can't offer. I looked down at her naked self as I stood next to the bed – trying to think of an excuse I could use to leave her. There were words coming out of her mouth, but I wasn't listening. Instead, I was looking at the mature female body that lay in front of me. What had she been like when she was young? I wondered. And then a vision of her daughter's naked body filled my mind and my blood boiled in an instant and bang!

She didn't have time to call for condoms that time. Then, after the race, I cuddled her and played all the games that she couldn't play with her vibrator.

"Can I ask you a question?" I asked.

"Go ahead," she said, "asking questions is what life is about."

"Did I get to you?"

"Yes, you got to me. You got to me better than my vibrator."

"You have a vibrator?" I asked, pushing surprise into my voice. "Nomsa, you are not the type! You really have a vibrator?"

"Yes, because a vibrator is honest," she said. "It is loyal, trustworthy and it will never desert any woman."

* * *

The next morning I woke up in her bed and later we shared a shower together. I was happy. This is the life, I thought. I have undressed the mother and her daughter. Life was good.

126

But she knew that I was having a sexual relationship with her child. "Can I tell you something?" she asked while we were eating breakfast together.

"Good or bad?"

"Bad. It is just a thought I had, so don't get mad, please."

I looked at her and nodded.

"For a moment there I thought you were having an affair with my child."

She had hit the mark, and suddenly my reactions were calculated because I didn't know how to handle her suspicion. "Huh!" I said. "You thought that about me?"

"I know, it's crazy, but it just came to me."

Nomsa should have listened to her heart, but instead she chose to be logical about the matter. "I understand why you might think that," I told her, realising that she had already dismissed the idea. "Most men are not trustworthy these days."

She was silent.

"Do you think that Reneilwe has a boyfriend?" I asked, knowing that I was safe. "I never thought that she was at that stage yet."

"She talks about boys," she replied, "and they are showing an interest in her." She paused. "Sometimes she even asks questions. It makes me uncomfortable. I mean, she is only twelve. It's scary. With Aids out there . . ."

"At twelve, I was playing like a toddler," Khutso said truthfully. "I only started to have sex at twenty-six."

* * *

I didn't want to see Nomsa again after that, but I had learned not to hurt the female heart in any way. It is always better to just push it away. "I think that we are too perfect," I told her one evening. "So perfect that I think we should get married."

"Married?"

I got down on my knees. "I want to continue living my life and you are the woman I want to live it with." I took a box out of my pocket and opened it. "Nomsa, will you marry me?"

She just stopped. Stopped breathing. Stopped everything. But I knew she would never agree to marry me. "No . . ." she started. "I . . ."

I was looking at her, pretending that I was deadly serious. "Nomsa, marry me," I said earnestly.

"Yes . . ." she said. "I mean, no . . ." She paused. "Listen to me first . . . I want to marry you, but I don't think it is the right thing for us to do. I have thought about it a thousand times, but then I remembered all the things that you said about your first marriage, about not being able to be a good husband. You said those things yourself, and when you said them I believed you."

Tears filled her eyes and she wiped them away. I wanted to cry too, but I couldn't, so I did the next best thing, I let my voice cry for me. "You don't love me," I said, flooding my voice with tears. "You want to use me as if I am your vibrator." I got up. "And you can't. I won't let you. I will not be your vibrator."

That last part, said with my voice filled with hurt and tears, was so convincing that I thought I deserved an Oscar.

"Khutso," she cried. "No, don't leave, I thought about marrying you, I did, but you told me yourself that you'll never be a good husband . . ."

Khutso said goodbye in the most gentlemanly of ways and walked away from her house. She was hurt, but we remained good neighbours, reinfecting each other whenever the opportunity arose.

* * *

When Reneilwe came back home for the next school holiday we had multiple sessions of reinfecting each other. By now she knew the race track very well, and I was sure that she had at least one other source of inspiration.

"I nearly slept with your mother," I told her.

"Why didn't you?" she asked. "She's lonely. You could have done it. You are a man, and all men are dogs."

"You think I should."

She nodded her head. "Anyway, I've got a boyfriend," she confessed, looking at me observantly. "I've got a boyfriend."

She saw the jealousy in my face. I couldn't hide it. "Jealous! Jealous!" she cried, pointing at me. "Well, stop it. You are my teacher and it is thanks to you that I am fucking his brains out. I am making him crazy."

\* \* \*

Later, I sat in the study looking at my distinguished book. On the 17th of July 2004 I had entered the name of the daughter: *Reneilwe* I remembered how I had carefully constructed every letter, hoping that somehow she would feel that she was being honoured with this entry in the greatest book of all. I looked at the group of letters that made up her name, once again wishing that she could experience this moment with me.

The name of the mother, *Nomsa*, was written underneath that of the daughter. I looked at both names, then I started to write underneath them. *Mother & daughter*, I wrote, *done*.

# Elizma

Liesel was a coloured woman Khutso had successfully defended. She had been charged with murdering her husband – in a fit of rage she had attempted to cut off his manhood while he was sleeping (earlier that same evening he had raped her and then beaten her up). That thing – curiosity, a fascination of some sort that attracts us to certain individuals – hit Khutso hard, and he knew he had to see her naked.

I thought that dinner would be a good starting point, but she stood us up. So then we – Khutso and I – decided to sit there by ourselves and just enjoy being us, something we didn't do much except when we had to use the toilet.

Three times the waitress had to take our order back to the kitchen to set it right. "I am very sorry, sir," she said as she put the food before me for the fourth time. "Please, try to enjoy the food."

Khutso looked at her. He was mad.

"I am very sorry . . ."

But, surprisingly, we enjoyed the food like we had never enjoyed food before.

Finally, I called for the bill, which she brought. "Thank you, sorry for the small inconvenience," she said respectfully. "You see . . ."

"No, don't explain, Elizma," I said, interrupting her. "Honestly, I enjoyed your food."

"That is my name, yes, how did . . ."

I pointed to her name tag. "Is a tip for good service or for good food?" I asked.

"Sorry, come again."

"I am wondering about tips. Are they for good service or for good food?"

"I think that it is for both good service and good food," she said. "I think they complement each other."

"And what if I had one and not the other?"

"Sir, you actually had both. You enjoyed the food because of the good service."

"Thank you, Elizma," I said, giving her a big tip.

"Thank you, sir."

*  *  *

Elizma was a third-year student at the University of Pretoria and we got to know each other well enough – she told the truth and got to know my lies.

One evening not long after the night at the restaurant she came over to my house and we shared a bottle of champagne. Halfway through the bottle the ice melted away and we started to kiss. For a black man like Khutso the sight of a light-complexioned black woman was enough to turn him on, and he couldn't wait to feel the thighs of a white woman. Suddenly, we were fighting her. "Ja, nog! Khutso, nog!" she said, defaulting to her mother tongue.

It was a dream come true for Khutso as he, like almost all black men, spent too much time looking at naked white women in newspapers, on TV and anywhere else he could find them. And here he was, not looking but having the real thing.

"Ag tog, man! Ag, man!" Elizma screamed.

Khutso thought of Tshepo covering his side of their room at university with posters of naked white women. At that moment he wanted to scream too, to call Tshepo to come and witness his triumph, and then he came, totally out of breath.

* * *

Khutso called Elizma. "Ek wil nie meer met jou praat nie," she said.

She broke Khutso's heart. He shook his head in disbelief, totally shocked.

"Ek wil nie meer met jou praat nie. Moet my nooit weer bel nie," she said.

Khutso tried to smile and laughed a little, but his heart wasn't in it.

"Hoor jy, moet my nooit weer bel nie," she said again and cut the call.

Honestly, Khutso was hurt. He wanted us to beg her – we had only been seeing her for a few days – but I thought it was better to let her go. After all, the job was done.

# II

Khutso went for an HIV test, just to check and see how far along we – Khutso and I – were:

> *Date: 06 January 2005*
> *Name: Khutso*
> *Age: 44 years*
> *Height: 1.74 metres*
> *Weight: 95.0 kilograms*
> *Status: HIV positive*
> *CD4 count: 400*

Afterwards, I told Khutso that he must save his life, not for himself but for the cause. He didn't like it. He did not want to take the treatment, but I forced him to. I had to remind him every time it was time to take the pills, but it was worth it.

ARVs. I like them. In fact, I love them. I want my soldiers to live as long as they can. I want them to have the freshest faces for the longest time, so that no one ever suspects that they are sick. That is the reason I love ARVs so much. And that is the reason I forced Khutso to take them.

# Sandra

I came back from work early one afternoon and found that there was a removal truck blocking my driveway. My good neighbours were on the move. On enquiry I found out that Nomsa had passed on. "Shame, my condolences," I said to her father. He was standing in the street, directing the removal. "She was such a good neighbour," I continued. "And little Reneilwe, how is she doing?"

"Reneilwe won't live long," the old man said with tears in his eyes. "A disease, a disease, my son . . . My heart breaks. Forget her mother, she had lived, but my Reneilwe, she is still a teenager, she has not seen the world yet."

"What can we do but let His will be done on earth as it is in heaven," I said, but the old man looked at me with eyes that asked "why do you talk of God when my children are dead?". "We are sorry to block your way," he finally said.

"It is nothing," I replied. "I am very sorry about your children."

I could not wait to get to my study, someone was dead and that had brightened my day immeasurably. Inside, I made straight for the book. Respectfully, I opened it at the mother-and-daughter page, then I filled in the empty column on the right-hand side with the words I had been longing to write for so long: *Dead. 30 January 2006.*

I was purring with pleasure at a job well done. This wasn't the kind of thing that happened on a daily basis, but it served as confirmation that I was finally getting the desired results, and having achieved something I needed to celebrate.

And what better way to celebrate than with another female that I had never been with before? It's hard to get a woman on demand in the suburbs, but it's an easy thing to do in the township. I called my pimps – by then I had pimps working for me in almost every township around Johannesburg – but as it was a Tuesday, they hadn't organised anything new for me. Only one of them was able to promise me something. "If I call you it means that I have something for you," he said. "But if you don't hear from me, then it means that it didn't come together."

Two hours later I had given up and was happily sitting in my study looking at my book, feeling fulfilled just by looking at it. Then my phone rang and I drove the hour-long drive that separated my exclusive neighbourhood from the inclusive neighbourhood where a seventeen-year-old – who had seen my cars several times and wondered about the man who drove them – was waiting impatiently to offer herself to me.

She was beautiful in a sort of rough ghetto way, and I could see the hope in her eyes. This rough ghetto beauty was hoping for a better life, she was sure better things were coming and that I was the one to bring them to her. She only had one condition: "You have to deliver me home before quarter to four," she said.

Apparently she had sneaked out of her mother's house and she had to sneak back in without anyone noticing.

She got into the front seat of my car and my pimp sat in the back. He wanted to use the car, so I let him take it after he had dropped us at a restaurant. We had seafood. She didn't like it much, but she pretended it was delicious. Then we took a taxi home.

Later, she wanted to say something about condoms, I could see it in her eyes, but she hesitated – she thought that it would spoil the fun if she did. The first round she was a dying sheep, it was very boring and

I thought it a poor way to celebrate great deeds, but the second round was fireworks – she was in it to win and I came hard. It disappointed her greatly, I could see it on her face, and it made me ashamed that I couldn't satisfy a seventeen-year-old girl.

Afterwards, Khutso decided that we had to clean ourself thoroughly. He drove around looking for a certain tree, but he couldn't find it around the city so we had to drive to the Lowveld where it grows in abundance. He boiled the sticks he had gathered and then we drank the mixture – four litres of it. The taste didn't go away for days.

After the mixture had passed through, I picked her up for a rematch, and we had countless rough ghetto sessions after that.

* * *

"My mother asked where I got the watch, the shoes, everything," she reported a few weeks later. "I told her and we talked about you. She wants to see you."

"She wants to see me?"

"Yes, she won't kill you. She just wants to see you."

"I don't know," I said. "What I will say to her?"

"Don't worry."

That was my cue to let go – I had achieved my purpose, after all – so I signed her into the holy book:

*30 January 2006: Sandra*
*You have just been conquered – blame it on your bad discipline.*

And then I forgot about her.

# Nonkululeko (Part 1)

Nonkululeko. Khutso thought that Nonkululeko was the reincarnation of Pretty. At twenty-three she had just joined the legal team of the broadcasting regulator. I thought that she would be a walkover, but I was wrong. She was different. She looked on men as fellow human beings, nothing more. In her world we were all sexless amoebas, and that was why what I thought was going to be a walkover became a two-year mission.

Nonkululeko had seen what I could do second-hand. She had watched her only brother die a slow, disgraceful death. Although she hadn't seen it right away – the truth about her brother's illness had been kept from her by her family – she had seen the disease take him down.

Her brother, Nkululeko, had been a strong young man with a big chest and a smile that disarmed every member of the female population he came across. He had been his mother's prince charming from the moment she had first held him in her arms, and she had never stopped pampering him – she had still been washing his socks and underwear, cleaning his room and making his bed when he was seventeen.

Nkululeko had a dozen girls. There were things about him that made every girl for miles around notice him, and it was rare that any girl said no to him. Of course, there were those who played hard to get, but Nkululeko never begged a girl. It was always the other way around: the girls begged him.

Nkululeko thought that he was knowledgeable, that he could outwit my forces, but what he didn't know was that he was already on the front line – and he stayed there for a full four years, a grade-A soldier working for me tirelessly night and day. Eventually his time came, the cracks had begun to show – the telltale signs of Aids entering its final stage – and I had to leave him because he was of no use to me any more.

One afternoon, not long after that, Nonkululeko arrived back home and suddenly felt that her family had changed somehow. She asked if something was wrong, but no one would answer her question. Then, a few days later, her mother suddenly began consulting with the very best of the local traditional healers – although they had never been a family that believed in traditional healing. It was all very strange.

MmaMamba was one of the best there was. It was rumoured that she could cure any disease, settle any dispute with the ancestors, break any curse and bring fortune and good luck. Because of this there was always a queue. First you queued to make an appointment, then you would be given a date when you would queue again to see mmaMamba. Nkululeko was given a date in two weeks' time, but one could always pay to jump the queue, and after money had changed hands they were asked to come back the following morning at five. In the meantime they were ordered not to drink, eat, wash or have sexual intercourse.

As her name suggests, to see mmaMamba one had to be naked. Her theory was that if people came to her naked she would be able to see their problems easily because the body exhibits everything that has happened to it since the day it was born. But what was truly unique about mmaMamba was that when you consulted with her you didn't have to explain your problems; she would tell you what was wrong. All you had to do was to question her if you didn't understand what she was telling you.

So, desperate for a cure for her son's illness, mother and son got naked with mmaMamba.

The healer looked at the naked mother and son. "Mother, you don't have any problems except for growing old." She paused and opened her eyes wide, giving the woman a chance to respond, but she didn't say anything, so she continued. "Your son," she said, pointing at Nkululeko with her fist, "he is eating your heart."

Nkululeko's mother felt the need to respond. "Yes, he is," she said.

"Because he is your only son, and though you think that you love both your children, you don't love your daughter as much as you love this son of yours, and he is troubling your heart."

"Yes."

MmaMamba looked at Nkululeko. "You are strong," she said. "I can't see you because you have the blood of kings."

"The blood of kings?" his mother asked.

"Your son is a king and there is a strong sangoma protecting him," mmaMamba replied.

"But this is the first time we have ever consulted a sangoma," his mother explained, puzzled.

"His sangoma runs in his blood, he is protecting your son," mmaMamba continued. "When was the last time you were sick?"

"I don't remember," Nkululeko said, but his mother knew that he had never been sick, not even as a child.

"It is because your blood is guarded," mmaMamba said. "I can try and ask whoever this sangoma is to let me see you, but I doubt that they would ever allow it. I can't help you."

* * *

Nkululeko's mother put her ear to the ground and listened. The ground told her of great healers, some of whom healed in the name of Jesus, others who healed with the power of the ancestors.

They went to one who healed the physically and mentally disabled in the name of Jesus. He touched Nkululeko's head, his hands shaking with the power of the Lord. "In the name of . . ." he said. Then he told them to believe that Nkululeko was healed.

Looking around, Nkululeko saw a crippled man let go of his crutches and walk slowly across the stage unaided. It was then that he believed. "Amen!" he shouted.

In the days that followed Nkululeko's healing, happiness returned to the family, but the next time Nkululeko took the test – this time he wasn't even a little scared – the results were even worse.

Again Nonkululeko looked at her family and felt the uneasiness within it. "What is going on, did somebody die?" she asked, half joking, but no one responded. Maybe, she thought, she should just let it be and whatever it was would pass. She was just making a big fuss over nothing, she told herself.

*   *   *

His mother took Nkululeko to another sangoma, one who claimed that he could clean the blood. There were many HIV-positive people in his yard, because he claimed that not one of his HIV-positive patients had ever died, but, ironically, Nkululeko's mother still believed that her son was not HIV positive: "We are just here to wash his bad blood," she said to one of the other patients.

Nkululeko could not say what was in the water because it looked and tasted like ordinary water, but after he had washed himself the water was dirty, as if he had washed with soap. He was asked to wash in the water again, and again there was dirt in the water, but by the end of his third bath there was less dirt, and after the fourth the water was relatively clean.

Then they ordered him to drink a five-litre bucket of the same water and vomit it out again. There was thick, brownish mucus with the first five litres, but by the third bucket the water came out as it went in – clean.

Then, finally, they brought out a three-litre douche can. They pumped three litres of water into his colon and he pushed it out. They repeated the process, but Nkululeko's energy began to go as they started with the third douche. The helpers didn't care. They were used to pushing the patients. They hurried everyone. "We don't have all day," they told Nkululeko. "And if you think that we aren't helping you, let us stop wasting each other's time."

At that moment Nkululeko felt like his life was worth nothing. He asked himself why his mother couldn't just let him die in peace.

After a week of doing the blood-cleansing rituals, he couldn't go on. "Ma, I'm sorry but I can't take this treatment any more," he said.

"Do you know how . . .?" his mother began, before choking on her words, tears filling her eyes. "Do you know how much I love you?" she finally asked, after she had composed herself. "Do you know how much I want you to live?"

And then Nkululeko felt that he had no choice but to endure the rituals for another week.

\* \* \*

When they got home after two weeks away, his father looked at them and told them that they needed to explain to Nonkululeko what was going on because she wasn't a child any more.

141

Nkululeko looked at her. "Nonkululeko," he said, "I am HIV positive."

"No, no, no," his mother said, contradicting her son. "He doesn't have Aids. He is bewitched, and because of that the sangomas can't see what is wrong with him." His mother paused to gather her breath. "People don't like us," she explained, her voice cracking as the tears came. "They have never liked my son. They have been trying to get to him from the day he was born, and now they have succeeded. But he won't die. No. He can't die. I won't let him die. People are jealous because he has a degree, because he has money, because he has a beautiful car. He has everything. And now we need to stand together and fight them . . ."

Nonkululeko looked at her brother, then at her father and finally at her mother. She had always been compared with Nkululeko, and at times she had tried to compete with him, but she had always fallen short. In fact, she had often hated her brother, not that she had wanted him dead, but . . . Tears started to fill her eyes. They were for her parents. She felt for them. They had always loved him more than they had loved her, and now he was going to die.

Nkululeko tried to dilute the tension. "Don't cry," he said, smiling. "It is just the way life is, smile and be happy."

But it didn't work. His father broke down in tears. He closed his eyes, as if trying to stop the tears, but the pain was too much and he bowed his head, shaking with suppressed grief. "Son . . ." he finally said. He took a long breath, swallowing the angry words that were bubbling up inside him. "Son . . ."

"Dad," Nkululeko said, interrupting him. "I am dying. It is a fact, I am dying."

"Son . . ." his father began again, but he couldn't go on with what he had to say. Standing, he pushed his chair back slowly and dragged himself wearily into the bedroom he shared with his wife.

142

Those were the last words their father ever said. The doctors said it was a stroke, and after four days in a coma he died.

* * *

What the doctors said about her husband's death didn't matter to their mother, she believed that what had happened was the result of the fact that her son was bewitched – there could be no other reason. Believing that they would still find a cure somewhere, she took him to Tshiane, in his world a renowned healer.

Tshiane looked hard at Nkululeko after he had consulted his trusted bones. "You have Aids," he said. "You are not bewitched. There is no-body after you. You have Aids. Do you know that, son? Do you know that you have Aids?"

Nkululeko admitted it.

The cure: during a full moon Nkululeko had to go and find a spot-less white female goat that had never given birth, then he must drink the potion that Tshiane had given him, have sex with the goat and then leave it to its fate. Following this, he mustn't talk to anybody un-til he had looked directly at the midday sun. "Then you must go and have another HIV test," Tshiane told him. "And only after you have seen the results can you come back and thank me for the service. You must pay what you think I deserve." He made a gesture that told them he was finished with them.

Nkululeko looked at his mother. "No, Ma, I won't do that," he said in front of the healer. "Just let me die."

She didn't say anything, but she went and found a spotless white goat.

"What is the goat for?" Nonkululeko asked.

"They say I have to have sex with that goat and it will heal me, get rid of this Aids inside me, but I am not going to do it. I refuse."

"Nkululeko, why can't you just do what Tshiane told you?" his mother asked him. "At least you will live. Son, please do as he said."

The goat did not stay too long with them before there was a full moon. Nkululeko's mother woke him up. "Leko, there is a full moon," she said.

"Mother."

"Nkululeko, do you think I am a witch?" she asked him, her tears already on their way. "Do you think that these things are easy for me?"

"Mother."

"Nkululeko, I want you to live. I am not asking you to disgrace yourself. I am asking you to save your life."

Tears filled his eyes as he looked at her.

"I know it is a hard thing for you to do," she continued, "but if you can't do it for yourself, then do it for me, son, do it for me."

"How can you ask me to do this?" Nkululeko asked her. "I am not having sex with any goat. Is it not enough that I am dying?"

"Leko," she pleaded. "Please."

\* \* \*

The need to live is a great force.

A crying goat interrupted Nonkululeko's dreams for a few seconds, then it made no more sound. She tried to nurse herself back to sleep, but curiosity dragged her out of her bedroom. In the back yard she saw that a rope had been tied around the goat's mouth so that it wouldn't cry out again as her only brother womaned it. Tears came to her eyes as she watched him with the goat, then she turned and walked back to her room.

\* \* \*

After the night of the full moon the family was destroyed. They couldn't even share a table any more. They couldn't look each other in the eye. It had made them strangers to each other, and, worst of all, Nkululeko still tested positive.

Finally, Nkululeko called them together. "Nonkululeko," he said, looking at his sister. "Ma," he said, looking at his mother. "I am very sorry for what has happened. I am dying, but I don't want you to die with me. You must continue living your lives. Ma, look at Nonkululeko, she still needs you, she loves you . . ." He tried to look into his mother's eyes, but she looked away.

It was no use. They couldn't even greet each other in the morning, and so they tried as best they could to avoid each other.

\* \* \*

Slowly Nkululeko's condition worsened until he had to leave his job. After that he remained in the house, getting weaker and weaker until he couldn't even get out of bed. His mother washed and fed him, but Nonkululeko couldn't even bring herself to go into his room.

Eventually, Nonkululeko could stand it no longer and mustered the courage to go into her brother's room. Opening the door, she looked at him where he lay, but he was barely recognisable. Her brother had had brown skin, expressive lips – that had the ability to put him into all kinds of trouble and talk him out of it again – and small shining eyes, sharp as an eagle's, but what was in the bedroom was something else. His eyes were huge, his skin pale and his lips had withdrawn from his teeth. Nonkululeko knew this scene, she had seen it many times before, but this was her own brother and she couldn't bear to look at him. "I am taking you to hospital," she said, looking away. "You have to get treatment."

145

Nkululeko was a typical black man. He hated the hospital – the hospital was a place to be born; it was for children – but he was too weak to fight Nonkululeko. They admitted Nkululeko immediately, believing that he was living on borrowed time – his viral load was very high, his CD4 count was below 100 and he had tuberculosis.

* * *

Nonkululeko looked at her phone. She saw the number and knew immediately that her brother was dead. Turning her phone off, she reversed out of her reserved parking bay and drove back home. Deep down inside she was relieved; her brother had finally found peace.

It took her two hours to drive to her mother's house, but when she arrived she did not find what she had expected. Nkululeko was still alive. It was her mother who had passed away. The maid had found her collapsed on the kitchen floor.

Three days before her mother's funeral, Nkululeko's body finally gave up the fight, and mother and son were buried on the same day.

At the funeral one could almost touch the anger, confusion and fear of the older generation, and it didn't help that the younger generation had come dressed to the nines to honour their Casanova, to celebrate Nkululeko's life one last time. To them he was just another one who had hit the jackpot, and they came dressed to impress. What is that expression, Khutso? Ah, yes, they came "dressed to kill".

* * *

So, having witnessed me in action Nonkululeko knew just what I could do. It wasn't something she had read about in the papers, or something she had heard positive people talk about their experiences of living with, it was something she knew. And that was why she wasn't willing

146

to put her life at risk by having sex. The whole experience had instilled in her a total fear of sexual intercourse so strong that it overwhelmed her womanly needs.

But I like a challenge, so I entered her in my divine book:

*15 May 2006: Nonkululeko*
*Age: 23*
*To be single for life (?)*

Nonkululeko became an experiment: to find out how resistant the female mind is and to prove to Khutso how much patience I have.

In the beginning we just talked and talked with Nonkululeko. We had lunches together. And slowly we became great friends.

For a year we had dinners together; we enjoyed plays, musicals and movies together; we attended concerts together. And during that year she slept at my house four times and never for a single second did she let her guard down. But after a year my patience ran dry, and I crossed her out of the great book:

*10 May 2007*
*Hard target. Some people are just as they want to be.*

# Nonkululeko (Part 2)

Despite the fact that I had failed to bed her, and had crossed her out of the book of books, Khutso took to calling Nonkululeko late at night when he couldn't sleep. They talked about everything under the sun, and eventually Khutso told Nonkululeko about Pretty, painting her perfectly. Then he told her about Thapelo, and how he had loved him too much.

It was then that she let down her guard for the first time. "My parents only loved my brother," she said.

"These are the complications of living," Khutso said. "But you are strong. You are a very strong woman, and that is why you are happy by yourself. You are happy with yourself and happy being yourself, and that is a quality that many women don't have, they need a man to validate their lives . . ."

I could hear her crying on the other end of the line.

"You shouldn't let it get to you," Khutso said. "It's made you the strong woman you are today."

*  *  *

Khutso got so close to Nonkululeko that he nearly opened up to her. He wanted to tell her the truth about our life. He felt an overwhelming need to relieve himself to her, but I restrained him.

"Do you ever think of getting married again?" she asked late one night.

"Yes, I do," Khutso replied.

"Why don't you?"

"The woman I want to marry doesn't want to get married. I love her very much, but we are happy as we are, marriage would complicate what we have."

She didn't respond.

"I am really happy with how things are," Khutso continued. "I . . ."

"How is your sex life?" she asked, interrupting him.

And it was at that moment that I knew that Khutso had done the impossible – he had got to her. "Do you really want to know?" I asked.

"Would I just ask?" she said. "You don't have to answer if you don't want to."

"I am not sure if this is what you want to hear, but you asked . . ." I said, trying to think of how I would address her in a way that would satisfy her. "After my wife died, I also wanted to die," I started. "It felt like there was no punishment worse than what I was going through. I dived deep into the bottle and I was happy there. I was always drunk." I paused to think of a way forward. "The prostitutes healed me," I finally said. "They showed me that I should appreciate my life, because however bad it was, it was far better than their lives. They opened my eyes, and I let go of the bottle and sobered up. After that I took sex into my mind. I masturbate twice a month, sometimes three times, just to relieve myself." I paused again. "Please, don't judge me."

"I am not judging you," she said, which was the truth, as I later found out that she had a collection of vibrators.

"It's silly, I know, but it has protected my life to this day," I said. "And these days I love to live. I want to turn one hundred and ten years old. For a long time I lived only to make money. It was, unfortunately, my only reason to live. But then I met my inspiration. You gave me a new reason to live."

I thought we had her then, but Khutso wasn't so sure and later on she expressed her fears to him – she wanted to believe my story, but there was another part of her that thought I might be lying.

"Well, a human being is a traceable thing," Khutso said. "All you have to do is hire a private detective and they will light up the dark spots for you."

Then I had to watch my back because I thought that she might just take Khutso's advice and investigate me. Khutso can be an idiot sometimes. Thankfully, she didn't. She thought we had nothing left to hide.

Finally, she was taken in. The continuity and unfaltering pace of the relationship had changed her mind, and she began to think about the things that a normal woman thinks about.

One evening we found ourselves back at my house and she let her guard down completely. We kissed and she exploded with pleasure. She couldn't control it. "Please, do me," she begged. "Do me."

"Aren't we moving too fast?" I asked.

"No," she said, purring with pleasure. "Please . . ."

Twice I talked her back to her senses, but the third time I let her have it.

*   *   *

Nonkululeko woke up in Khutso's bed, naked and a little worried, but we washed away her worries with a morning session.

"I am happy," she said afterwards, but she looked worried. There were questions in her mind that she wanted to ask, so then I left a fake HIV-test certificate lying around so that she would see it, and after that she really was happy.

I re-entered her in the distinguished book on a new page:

*Miraculously done. Who said that patience and hard work don't pay off.*

Then I cursed myself with pride. "I am a shit of a man," I said and smiled. "I am a dangerous motherfucker!"

\* \* \*

"I am pregnant," Nonkululeko announced happily.

"You're pregnant?" I asked, a billion negative thoughts attacking my mind.

She paused her celebrations as she read my body language. "Yes," she said.

"You are pregnant?" I asked again, trying to pretend to be excited.

"I said 'yes'."

"You are . . ."

\* \* \*

Later, I showed up at her town house with a bunch of flowers. "I have always wanted you," I said. "The day I saw you I wanted to marry you, and I still do. Can I marry you?"

I got down on my knees and took out the box that a couple of women had seen before. "Nonkululeko, I love you. Can I marry you?" I asked, taking the diamond ring out of its box.

Then the happy feeling that I had destroyed earlier came back and there were joyful tears. "Yes," she cried. "Yes, I want to marry you."

But a couple of months later everything was spoiled. She failed a routine HIV test. It was a TKO – she fell flat in the fight of life.

All evidence pointed to me, so she drove to my place in a rage and shoved the certificate in my face. She started to hit me as hard as she could, but I didn't care, I just let her hit me until she ran out of steam and sank down onto the floor in a river of tears. You were on the right track all along, I wanted to tell her, but your weakness is the fact that you are a woman.

I took an HIV test that afternoon, then I drove over to her town house with the fake negative certificate and the real positive one. "Look!" I said, pretending to be angry. "You want to explain this? Four months ago I was HIV negative, then I slept with you, and look what I have now."

I moved towards her as if I was going to hit her the way she had hit me, but I never raised my hand. You are dying, baby, I thought. Then Khutso left her.

*  *  *

The truth is that everybody thought the strain of losing her parents and brother in the same year was just too much for her heart to handle. I just smiled and filled in the empty column next to her name:

*Died: 07 June 2008*
*Cause of death: suicide*

# III

The great book became our whole world, and at times I even felt like Khutso's job was a big hindrance to the cause – if he hadn't been working I would already have been much bigger than I was. The average entry was seven women a week, one for each day of the week, but the record was sixteen in a week: 23-29 June 2003. That was when Khutso was at his peak. We were dangerous then. How? Money and women. They mix in ways that even I don't understand. And Khutso, well, he had enough money, and he could kick it the way he liked.

# Daisy Fay

I was cruising in Khutso's British supercar – prowling, top down, along Oxford Road on my way to Rosebank. A Gwyneth Paltrow lookalike was cruising next to me in her convertible and I was loving it. Suddenly, a G-string hit me in the face and fell into my lap. I looked at Gwyneth and caught her naughty smile.

I picked the G-string off my lap and smelled it. She had just taken it off – it was wet and covered in her scent. I kissed it, looking at her, and then we nearly caused traffic.

Further down Oxford Road I threw my cellphone into her car, then called it with my car phone. "Smells good," I said. "Can I taste it?"

"Is that how black men do their thing?" she asked.

"I'm not sure about black men, I am not representing any black men," I replied. "I am talking to you and you are talking to me."

"Where are you going, black man?"

"White woman, this black man is just out walking his machine. And what are you up to, white woman? Can I . . ." I paused.

"Can you what, black man?"

"Can I taste it?"

"You don't sound sure you want to," she said. "Are you scared? Do I scare you?"

"White woman, do you want to scare this black man?"

I was definitely not her first black catch. I was part of a game that she was playing with affluent black men, and that thought made me try and stop myself from coming. I wanted her to be the first one of us to raise the white flag, but eventually I couldn't hold out any more. I was disappointed because I knew that I wouldn't see her again – that wasn't part of her game.

She told Khutso that her name was Daisy Fay, but when he was signing her into the book of books he remembered that Daisy Fay was a character in a novel he had read. Still, he signed her in anyway:

*15 August 2008: Daisy Fay*
*Done. Liberal white woman!*

# Kgahliso

Pretty's younger sister Kgahliso came to the city of gold and wanted to see Khutso. Every now and then they had had a telephonic conversation, but the last time she had seen him in person was at her sister's funeral. She liked to be nosey about her sister's old man and was always pushing Khutso to marry again. "Honestly, Khutso, if you had died my sister would have got herself another man, and that wouldn't have meant that she didn't love you," she would say. "You have to get yourself a wife, and on my sister's grave, she will rest in peace knowing that you are being taken care of."

"Traditionally, I am supposed to marry you," Khutso had said the first time she had said this, "but you are already married."

"Khutso, we are not living in the past," she had replied. "You need to get married."

Though she was in the city on business, she came to visit us, just to nose around, asking this and that about her in-law.

But it wasn't long before she became a nagging mosquito. "Khutso," she said. "You didn't come to your brother's funeral. I understand that, but you didn't bury your own mother. You didn't come to my father's funeral. What is going on?" Tears filled her eyes. "And worse . . . worse than all of that, you haven't seen your son since . . . Well, you know when. You didn't even come to see him when he finished his initiation. What is going on with you?"

I turned and looked the other way, trying to fill my eyes with tears. "Kgahliso, I am hurting," I said. "I need help."

She moved closer, wiped away my tears and gave me a hug. "Khutso, you have to deal with it," she said. "You can't just run away . . ." She paused. "Khutso, you lost somebody you loved, but Thapelo lost that person too. All he has is you. He needs you . . ."

Khutso managed to let a few tears run from his eyes. Kgahliso wanted to comfort him, and then this led to that and it wasn't long before we were running the Comrades Marathon – comfort sex.

As for her, Khutso thought that it was probably something that had been on her mind for many years, from long before Pretty had died – she wanted to feel what it was like to be Mrs Khutso.

*　*　*

Kgahliso stayed for two nights. After she had left, I went to the study and picked up my favourite book and began to page through it, looking at all the names I had entered into it.

There are people who claim this and that about women, but my book was proof that I had slept with all these women. Then I thought that I should have written their contact numbers down next to their names, so that if even one dumb man disputed what I claimed he could call them and confirm the facts.

If they were still alive, and willing to testify, these women would tell you about a man who showered them with all sorts of expensive gifts and took them on countless weekends away. They would tell you about this guy that some of them got to know as Khutso, but most knew as Moleko because of the personalised registration plates on Khutso's cars – Moleko 1 (the Voroso), Moleko 2 (the convertible) and Moleko 3 (the British supercar). They would tell you that Moleko loved them like nobody had ever loved them, but only for a short while. Moleko, who left without saying goodbye, because he didn't want to break their fragile hearts. Moleko, who they still hope will come back for them.

I paged through the full pages, smiling at the names of the ones that I knew had passed on, slowly caressing the writing with my fingers as I wondered about some of the others. The book was nearly full, only four blank pages remained, and Khutso thought that he needed to place another order with the printer so that he could begin the second instalment of the *Book of the Dead*.

Finally, on the next blank page I wrote:

*28 September 2008: Kgahliso*
*You are dying soon. Won't you tell your sister that I am not mad at all.*

Then I put my shoeless feet up on the table, closed my eyes and smiled. This is what personal satisfaction is – knowing that after all your hard work your purpose has been fulfilled. These are the small moments that make life worth living; moments that one can't share with anyone else, moments that make me want to scream: "Life is good!"

# Thapelo

Thapelo. After Kgahliso's visit, Khutso invited the little gangster to come and spend the school holidays with his father. I was reluctant. I didn't want to pick him up at the airport, but eventually Khutso persuaded me.

Khutso wasn't sure that he would recognise Thapelo, but in the end he picked him out easily. He saw a younger version of himself come through the sliding doors at the airport and immediately he got angry. Anger gripped him and he could not move. He despised Thapelo. Eventually, I had to intervene. I approached the boy and as we drew closer Khutso decided that he wanted to give him a hug, but then the little gangster looked up at him and he lost his nerve. Khutso hesitated as Thapelo looked down at his luggage, avoiding our eyes. He wasn't comfortable either. "Dad?" the little gangster asked.

Then Khutso stepped forward and gave Thapelo the hug he had intended to give him, the commotion of the airport receding as Khutso and the little gangster tried to fill the six cold, empty years with a hug. "Thapelo. I am sorry, my son," Khutso said. "I love you."

That brought them back to reality, and the little gangster wiped a tear from the corner of his right eye. "Dad, you are embarrassing me," he said, picking up his luggage.

*　*　*

In the car on the way back to the house the little gangster remained silent, but Khutso couldn't hide his excitement. "Thapelo," he said, looking at him as they left the car park, "how was your flight?"

"Bumpy," Thapelo replied. "I didn't know that there were bumps in the air, but I know now. It was an experience."

We drove on in silence, Khutso smiling like I had never seen him smile before.

*  *  *

The following day, Khutso offered the little gangster the opportunity of driving one of his cars. "Pick a car, son," he said.

The little gangster picked Moleko 3, so Khutso called a race circuit and they spent two hours together there. Khutso taught the little gangster how to drive a supercar and it wasn't long before he was pushing it fearlessly, scaring his father. Driving together washed away all the tension and began to bridge the six-year gap. They were almost happy, father and son.

"Dad, can I hug you?" Thapelo asked when they had finished driving.

Then he hugged us, the little gangster, and it made Khutso truly happy.

"Sometimes, what a boy needs is a hug from his father, especially if he doesn't have a mother," the little gangster said, tears filling his eyes. "But if his father has become an ATM it's hard to get a hug. It's hard to hug an ATM, Dad."

I wanted to tell the little gangster that we were too busy to check up on him all the time, but Khutso stopped me.

"Can you stop doing whatever it is that is so important in your life, Dad?" Thapelo continued. "Can you stop for five minutes and take a look at my life?"

Khutso didn't know what to say.

"Dad, there are all kinds of dangers in the world: drugs, crime, HIV/

Aids. And I am living amongst all these things alone. Do you care about me at all?"

I knew then that the little gangster would one day make a formidable soldier in my legion, and all that he needed to know was that his mother had committed suicide because she had discovered that she was HIV positive.

"Dad, you don't know how hard it is to live with my aunt," Thapelo went on. "The only time I am happy is when I am at school. There we are all boarders and everyone is an orphan till there is a parents' meeting or a sports day."

"I am very sorry, son," Khutso said. "And believe me, I want to make it right, I really do want to make it right, but, Thapelo, I am afraid it is too late."

I stopped Khutso there. He wanted to disclose more than was necessary. Khutso, I told him, patting him on the shoulder, you don't want to hurt this boy any further by telling him that he is going to lose you too, he's hurting as it is.

*　*　*

Somehow Khutso found a way to mend their relationship, and after three days together he and the little gangster were hugging each other as if they had never been apart.

"Dad, do you think that Mom misses us?" the little gangster asked him on the evening of the third day.

"I think that she misses us," Khutso replied.

"Do you miss her?"

"A lot," Khutso lied.

"It is funny because I don't miss her at all, and that is the saddest thing about my life. You don't have any idea how much it hurts me that

161

I don't miss her at all, Dad. I feel like I am an animal." He paused. "When you miss her, what do you miss about her?" he asked.

"All the love that she had for us," Khutso said lamely.

Silence fell.

"What is your dream car, son?" Khutso finally asked.

"I don't have a dream car," the little gangster replied. "I don't dream, Dad, I have goals, and the most important thing about my goals is that they have a time limit, something that dreams don't have. That way I know that I have to work hard to achieve my goal before its expiry date."

We – Khutso and I – were impressed by the little gangster's little sermon. Khutso laughed, feeling like a fool because he had always had dreams and they had never had an expiry date. "What is your goal car then?" I asked.

So Thapelo told his father about his car.

"But that's a student car," Khutso said. "I thought you were going to give me the name of a supercar."

"Yes, Dad, I know, but I am still in high school, those cars aren't part of my goals yet." Then the little gangster smiled knowingly – he had us where he wanted us. "They will be in time," he said, "when I take aim for them."

Khutso laughed it off, blooming with pride.

\* \* \*

"Dad, are you going to marry again?" Thapelo asked the following evening, when we were having a supper of takeaway chicken, chips and rolls.

"No," Khutso answered. "I won't get married again."

"Do you have a girlfriend?"

"No, do you?"

162

"I have a couple of girlfriends," Thapelo replied.

"But aren't you afraid of Aids?" I asked the little gangster.

"Who isn't, Dad?" he said. "I am terrified of Aids. But guess why I broke up with my ex's?"

"Why did you break up?" I asked.

"Because I wouldn't sleep with them."

I was disappointed, though in truth I didn't believe him – I didn't want to believe him.

"I am terrified of Aids. I hate Aids, Dad, I hate it," the little gangster continued. "If Aids were a person, I would kill him or her with my bare hands, but there is no Aids, there are only people, and that is the worst thing about Aids."

True, there is no Aids, only people, I thought, listening attentively.

"Do you know how many suicides we have had at school this year?" he asked me, knowing full well that I had no idea. "Four. And that was after a girl who was sleeping around died an HIV-related death . . ."

"Thapelo, you just keep on abstaining," Khutso told the little gangster, even though he hurt me by saying it.

"But I can't abstain for the rest of my life, can I?" Thapelo said. "No, I can't, and that is the worst thing, because once I take off my underwear it's like putting my head in a hangman's noose and waiting for the ground to give way beneath my feet, all the time hoping that it doesn't. I don't trust my girlfriends, but I am a hypocrite because I have three of them: one at home, one in Polokwane and one at school. I am also untrustworthy. And once I start sleeping with them, I will be putting my head in the hangman's noose, and one day the ground will surely give way and I will hang. There is no way around it, Dad. Or is there?"

He looked at me, hoping that I would be able to give him some kind of an answer, but Khutso had nothing to say. I smiled. I am coming for you, little gangster, I thought quietly to myself. You are right, there is no way around it.

* * *

When the time came for the little gangster to go back to school it was a sad goodbye and Khutso cried. I was also sad. I liked the little boy. I liked him because I knew that one day he would make a formidable soldier in my legion.

# IV

The last golden page of the *Book of the Dead* is, just like the first page, dedicated to Khutso for the remarkable work he has done for this cause:

*06 November 2008: Khutso*
*Age: 47 years*
*Height: 1.74 metres*
*Weight: 65.0 kilograms*
*CD4 count: 60*

It was an honour knowing you, I tell him. I have had great soldiers, I have seen their great deeds, but you, you come second to none. But now, Khutso, your time is done, I tell him. You are dying and I have to move on, I have to find another soldier of the highest grade.

It is always sad to say goodbye. It fills me with shame that I have to leave him, but death is hovering like a hungry vulture. You are done, I tell him, patting him on the shoulder. I wish I could save him. I wish that we could go on working together forever, but that isn't possible. Khutso, thank you. Here is where we – you and I – take different paths.

For the last time I touch the great book, thinking of all the triumphs we have shared, then I put it down and get up and walk away before the tears come. Somewhere out there I have conquered another author of no mean talent, and we are starting another book together for the cause.

"Aids is no longer just a disease, it is a human rights issue."

NELSON MANDELA

Personifying + rationalizing AIDS → process, rules to the game, human agency

↓

Parallel for charisma

↓

darkest metaphor to capture violence of charisma → death

↓

charisma encourages/ forces SD

KGEBETLI MOELE was born in Polokwane and raised on a family farm. His first novel, *Room 207*, was published to great critical acclaim in 2006. It was short-listed for the Commonwealth Writers' Prize for the Best First Book in Africa in 2007, joint winner of both the Herman Charles Bosman Prize and the University of Johannesburg Debut Fiction Prize, and one of the four titles that received honourable mention by the judges of the Noma Award for Publishing in Africa, also in 2007.

Kgebetli lives in Tshwane.